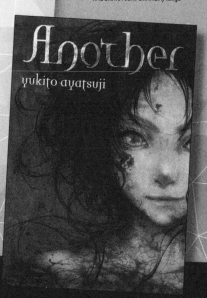

Magical Girl Raising Project

restart 1

Asari Endou

Illustration by
Marui-no

CLANTAIL
Can transform the lower half of her body into different animals.

PECHKA
Can create really delicious food.

NONAKO MIYOKATA
Can make friends with any animal.

RIONETTA
Can manipulate dolls with her thoughts.

PFLE
Uses a magical wheelchair to race at intense speeds.

MAGICAL GIRLS

NOKKO
Can change the feelings of those around her.

MAGICAL DAISY
Can shoot lethal Daisy Beams.

@MEOW-MEOW
Can trap things inside paper talismans.

GENOPSYKO YUMENOSHIMA
Can block any attack with her magical suit.

MASKED WONDER
Can change any object's weight.

SHADOW GALE
Can power up machines by modifying them.

DETEC BELL

Can talk to buildings.

CHERNA MOUSE

Can make herself really big.

LAPIS
LAZULINE

Can use gems
to teleport.

MELVILLE

Can change her color at will.

AKANE

Can cut anything
she sees.

MAGICAL
GIRLS

2

Asari Endou

Illustration by Marui-no

YA

NEW YORK

Magical Girl Raising Project, Vol. 2
Asari Endou

Translation by Alexander Keller-Nelson and Jennifer Ward
Cover art by Marui-no

"MAHO SHOJYO IKUSEI KEIKAKU restart (first part)" by Asari Endou, Marui-no
Copyright © 2012 Asari Endou, Marui-no
All rights reserved.
Original Japanese edition published by Takarajimasha, Inc., Tokyo.

English translation rights arranged with Takarajimasha, Inc. through Tuttle-Mori Agency, Inc., Tokyo.

English translation © 2017 by Yen Press, LLC

Yen On
1290 Avenue of the Americas
New York, NY 10104

Visit us at yenpress.com
facebook.com/yenpress
twitter.com/yenpress
yenpress.tumblr.com
instagram.com/yenpress

First Yen On Edition: November 2017

Yen On is an imprint of Yen Press, LLC.
The Yen On name and logo are trademarks of Yen Press, LLC.

The publisher is not responsible for websites
(or their content) that are not owned by the publisher.

Library of Congress Cataloging-in-Publication Data
Names: Endou, Asari, author. | Marui-no, illustrator. |
Keller-Nelson, Alexander, translator. | Ward, Jennifer, translator.
Title: Magical girl raising project / Asari Endou ; illustration by Marui-no ;
translation by Alexander Keller-Nelson and Jennifer Ward.
Other titles: Mahâo Shâojo Ikusei Keikaku. English
Description: First Yen On edition. | New York, NY : Yen On, 2017–
Identifiers: LCCN 2017013234 | ISBN 9780316558570 (v1 : pbk) | ISBN 9780316559911 (v2 : pbk)
Subjects: | CYAC: Magic—Fiction. | Computer games—Fiction. |
Social media—Fiction. | Competition (Psychology)—Fiction.
Classification: LCC PZ7.1.E526 Mag 2017 | DDC [Fic]—dc23
LC record available at https://lccn.loc.gov/2017013234

ISBNs: 978-0-316-55991-1 (paperback)
978-0-316-56013-9 (ebook)

1 3 5 7 9 10 8 6 4 2

LSC-C

Printed in the United States of America

CONTENTS

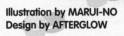

Go ahead!!

What Is *Magical Girl Raising Project*?

☆ Simple and fun for beginners, yet deep enough to keep experts addicted!
★ Features Magical Trace System controls that feel just like real life!
☆ Amazing, ultrarealistic graphics!
★ An ever-increasing library of items to get your collector's spirit burning!
☆ Completely free to play! No purchase required—ever!

Magical girls, welcome to a world of swords and fantasy!

We're relaunching *Magical Girl Raising Project* as a mobile game specifically for magical girls. Strengthen your friendships with your allies and face powerful enemies with your abilities! You'll need strength, kindness, knowledge, and courage in order to have a chance of surviving in this game.

Your goal is to progress through the world, unlocking new areas as you go. By the time you've defeated the Evil King lurking in the deepest depths of the game, you'll have grown as a magical girl—and in real life. That's the educational and training simulator element of this super RPG.

Work together with your fifteen allies to take down the Evil King and bring peace to the world!

- Objective: to defeat the Evil King
- Completion reward: ten billion yen—but only to the player who lands the finishing blow
- Area unlock award: one million yen—but only to the players who unlock them
- Participation award: one hundred thousand yen—received even in the case of a game over

PROLOGUE

"Daisy! It's that warehouse!" Palette shouted, head sticking out of the *pochette* hanging from Daisy's waist.

The warehouse the creature pointed at was noticeably shorter and older than the surrounding structures, and rather mysterious. But Magical Daisy, who knew what was going on inside, could find it only grotesque.

She ran, weaving between the buildings, kicking off one to launch herself onto another and bound away again, leaping and springing along. Today, there would be a drug deal inside this storehouse on the outskirts of the downtown area. The Magical Kingdom had ordered Daisy to raid the storehouse, apprehend the perpetrators, and then report back. Daisy leaped off the side of another edifice and did a half spin in midair, the wind between the buildings battering her cheeks and furiously ruffling her hair, skirt, and accessories. Upside down in the air, she pointed her finger at the storehouse.

"Let's do this! Daisy Beam!"

Magical girls were a type of mage: people granted power by the Magical Kingdom who used their gifts for the good of the

world and for humanity—and for themselves, just a little bit. Their physical abilities exceeded biological limits, and the mystic phenomena at their fingertips defied the laws of nature.

Through the ages, many systems of power had relied on magic or miracles: churches, heresy, alchemy, devil worship, folk beliefs, and others. The Magical Kingdom, a utopia of dreams and fantasy, had always cooperated with these organizations in an effort to bring about world peace. In the modern day, they had created the revolutionary subculture that is magical girls. Kind, lovely, beautiful, and strong of heart, these guardians never gave up their mission to protect people. The notion spread far and wide, and more and more girls, boys—and in some cases, even adults—came to idolize magical girls, creating a breeding ground for cultivating potential and actual allies of the Magical Kingdom.

These heroines never revealed themselves. They surreptitiously took root in society and daily life, their activities hardly ever rising to the surface—though the use of the term "hardly ever" naturally meant that it did happen, albeit rarely. There were occasional incidents, but the Magical Kingdom took care of them quietly, altering the memories of those involved, as well as falsifying any government records to make it seem as if nothing had ever happened.

Aside from the "accidents," there was also publicity. The activities of some magical girls were dramatized, altered, and then distributed as anime and manga. A surprising number of people had either received the blessings of the Magical Kingdom or were its citizens working in this world, and they had considerable sway over production companies and television stations. Normal viewers enjoyed the creative content, never realizing the stories were based on true events. As for the girls, the true heroines, their hearts filled with pride.

Magical Daisy, a television anime that had originally aired years earlier, was one such production. In the show, a magical princess from the World of Flowers transfers to a school in modern-day Japan and causes quite a stir. While normally, she appears to be the kind of middle school student one would find anywhere, when trouble occurs, she transforms into Magical Daisy. Daisy and her sidekick, Palette, are allies of justice, beating the bad guys and helping those in need. However, no one could ever know her true identity, because if that happened, she'd be forced to return to the World of Flowers.

The anime *Magical Daisy* was based off the activities of a real magical girl. Her being a princess and transferring to a Japanese school was fiction, but the rest generally stuck closely to the source.

Somewhere, a dog was howling.

A drunk lay passed out spread-eagle in the middle of the alley. When Magical Daisy picked him up, the stench of alcohol stung her nose. He muttered nasty things to her, like "You got a problem with me?" and "You piece of shit!" but he was basically talking in his sleep. He wasn't aware of himself.

She searched through the leather bag that she presumed was his and pulled his license out of his wallet. She checked his address, hoisted him over her shoulder, and dashed off toward his home. Once there, she laid him at the front door and rang the doorbell.

A middle-aged woman, probably his wife, shouted from inside, "Where the hell were you?!"

Now Magical Daisy's mission was complete, but she'd only managed to help one person. She hadn't completed her quota for the night. Next, she would head downtown and patrol. After scouring the area to make sure there was no trouble, no disputes, she would finally head home.

She hopped on the train from her university, and in fifteen minutes, she was in the downtown district under her care. From there, it was four stations and hardly a five-minute walk to her cheap, one-story apartment building—basically a town house—in her quiet, residential neighborhood. In one of these rooms was Kiku Yakumo's home.

Her ceiling, barely thicker than plywood, was sand-textured plaster that would break with a single strike. Her bathroom had a traditional squat toilet, and if she wanted to wash, she went to the neighborhood bathhouse. But worst of all, her landlord was a jerk—a judgmental, gossipy nag. Kiku lived there only because the rent was cheap.

"I'm home."

Habits formed over many years didn't change overnight, and her voice echoed in the empty room. The walls were as thin as you could get, so the other tenants around her had probably heard. Maybe her neighbors thought she was lonely.

She couldn't argue with that assessment.

Taking two pieces of chewing gum from the plastic case on the low table, she popped them in her mouth and started chewing. She tossed her school tote bag onto her folded-up futon, sat next to it, and sighed. Feeling about ready to collapse, she leaned back on her arms.

Back in middle school, during her heyday as Magical Daisy, she'd always had so much fun. In high school, she'd resolved every major case, and eventually, her sidekick, Palette, had returned to the Magical Kingdom. The two of them must have shed nearly a gallon's worth of tears the day they parted ways. Kiku wouldn't have denied being lonely, but she'd still been able to text Palette with her magical phone, and *Magical Daisy* was being adapted into an anime. Daisy had no idea what kind of connections the Magical Kingdom had in her world, but the story in the anime had reflected reality quite closely. Despite its relatively average popularity, the show had received decent reviews and continued in a second season, released as an OVA. While she was working hard on her patrols, Kiku had also often gleefully posted on the *Magical Daisy* forums online and checked sales data on tracking sites.

Then she'd started university.

Kiku had ended up in a very average university. She might have been able to aim for a better one if she'd studied harder, but prioritizing her magical-girl activities hadn't left much time for schoolwork. As a defender of justice, she couldn't skip out on training, patrolling, and beating bad guys.

She'd stopped talking to her friends from middle and high

school, and there was no one at her university she might call a friend. It wasn't uncommon for her to leave the house and come back without having uttered a single word.

Her living situation was terrible. Her magical-girl activities took up most of her time, meaning she couldn't work a part-time job. Her family ran a small workshop in town, and because of the recession, they were just barely scraping by. Kiku was grateful to even receive an allowance. Her clothes all came from big wholesalers, though lately she hadn't bought any. She didn't know the first thing about makeup. She had no qualifications. She didn't even have a driver's license. These were all things she'd considered unnecessary as a magical girl, and she was fine with that. In private, she suffered, but out in the world, she kept up with her supernatural responsibilities. To Kiku, that was what it meant to be a hero.

But lately, she was starting to question the role. The life of her alter ego didn't have that same glow it'd had in middle school—this secretive heroism where she had to carefully avoid showing herself to anyone. Apparently, there had been some experimental trials that used curated sites and the like to publicize the existence of magical girls a little more, but thanks to a certain series of events, the project had fizzled out. Kiku continued her low-key activities, evading the public eye, sneaking, hiding, never receiving any praise or thanks from the people she helped.

If only she'd studied a little more. Goofed off a little more. Worn fancy clothes, gotten boys to talk to her. Kiku had never even done karaoke before. She wanted to try bowling, too. Where was her future headed? How long would she be a magical girl? Doubts filled her mind as she helped people in need.

It was starting to rain, and she could hear the droplets splashing against the corrugated roof. She hated that sound; it represented exactly how tough her life had become. As she heaved another deep sigh, her magical phone began playing the opening theme to *Magical Daisy* to alert her to a new message.

Was it a whiny text from Palette? Or possibly an emergency

message from the Magical Kingdom? She shuffled across the tatami mats on her knees, grabbed the magical phone, and opened her inbox.

"*Magical Girl...Raising Project?*" That sounded familiar. Kiku could've sworn she'd heard of a similar mobile game before. Was it an advertisement for the game, then? Or some kind of prank? She decided it was best to delete it and tapped the button to do so.

"...Huh?" But she couldn't. She tried pressing harder, thinking the touch screen might be screwy, but nothing happened. The words scrolled smoothly down, ignoring her input. After a few blocks of explanatory text, the final line of the e-mail hit the screen.

The game will now begin.

Kiku squinted as the plain serif typeface suddenly radiated with all the colors of the rainbow.

CHAPTER 1
HELLO, DAISY

☆ **Pechka**

During her work as a magical girl, she'd been spotted a few times. The rule of thumb was to keep hidden and act in secret, but if a very young child—someone who wouldn't see them as an oddity—happened to catch a glimpse, there was an unspoken understanding that there was nothing much to be done about it, though it was frowned upon.

Summer was at its peak. In the early afternoon at the park, the asphalt was practically softening in the heat. Cicadas hummed hoarsely, and mothers buzzed merrily with the latest gossip.

A girl of about kindergarten age, possibly waiting for her mother, was squatting in the shade, out of the harsh sunlight. In her right hand, she held a thin white string connected to a floating red balloon with a drugstore logo imprinted on it. The light filtering through the trees produced a mottled pattern on the rubber as it bobbed lazily in the air.

Suddenly, the wind picked up. The girl covered her eyes with her right hand—the one holding her balloon. The gust jerked the string from her grip, and with an "Oh!" she looked up to see her prize rising straight into the blue sky. The girl's look of surprise disappeared, replaced by welling tears.

Then, as if from nowhere, a magical girl dashed forward, leaped high into the air, and snatched the lost balloon. She handed it to the little girl with a smile and a "Here you go." The magical girl would have been more careful had she been helping an adult, but she figured it was fine to give a child an extra smile.

"Thank you!" the child shouted excitedly, a big smile on her face. "Miss…you're so pretty." She was entranced.

The magical girl, Pechka, responded with a sloppy grin and then quickly hid herself to make sure none of the mothers nearby spotted her. A magical girl's outfit stuck out like a sore thumb, making it especially harrowing to work while the sun was up. "Swift and nimble" was the creed in daytime.

Yes, for Chika Tatehara, the ability to transform into a beautiful girl was more important than any added magic or physical prowess. It was fair to say that her appearance accounted for 70 percent of the reason she was in this business.

Chika was not a fan of her natural looks. She had moles all over, and she was certain her nose pointed too far upward. Her right and left breasts didn't match in size or shape. Her fingertips were thick and round. She was so bowlegged that her legs never touched. No matter how much milk she drank, she was still short. And her eyes could stand to be bigger. No one had ever called her ugly, but neither could she recall ever hearing the words "cute" or "pretty" applied to her. She had a feeling that people purposefully avoided talking about her appearance. Perhaps that was something of a victim complex on her part, but maybe it wasn't just her imagination after all.

In middle school, Chika had avoided anything that drew attention, trying to be as average as possible. Even if no one ever praised her, at least no one ever put her down, either. She'd spent her whole life thus far maneuvering in this way.

She'd never considered it a bad thing. Relative obscurity had its own joys, after all. She could play games and use the cute photo booths at the arcades that school rules forbade students from visiting, or she could read and share naughty books with a book club. Sure, it wasn't what those girls with gobs of mascara did, but she could still get up to no good.

But there were some things Chika couldn't do.

Ninomiya, number four on the baseball team, was outstandingly talented—their star player and cleanup batter, who had pro scouts all over him and a career in the major leagues all but in the bag. He had a calm and carefree personality, and he enjoyed baseball, eating, and sleeping. On first glance, his height and weight would suggest he was much older than middle school, and most people found him frightening upon first meeting, but he was pleasant and all smiles in conversation. His quick grins and talent for baseball attracted girls not just from his own school but from nearby middle schools, high schools, and even universities. They all came running to cheer him on not only for games but even for practices.

As a huge fan of Ninomiya, Chika was no exception. She often made excuses about it, telling herself that she was different from those other superficial fans. She just loved baseball and watching him play. His slider pitches in particular were on another level, like magic.

After matches and practice, girls would rush over carrying offerings for him: towels, candied lemons, kettles of cold water, and so on. Due to an unspoken rule, the girls would line up in order of attractiveness. If Chika were to push others aside on the approach, the next day, they'd be talking behind her back and spreading rumors to make her an outcast. It would have painted the rest of her middle school days black.

But what would life be like if she were pretty? What if she were as beautiful as a pop idol or a model? Then no one would object.

No one would be *able* to object. She wished so badly to get close to Ninomiya, for him to eat a homemade lunch she'd put her heart into, that she wanted to become someone else. The offer of magical girlhood was a godsend for someone with such a desperate desire to be beautiful. She did her damnedest to pass the selection test and become the magical girl Pechka.

And now, looking at herself in the mirror, Chika breathed a sigh. Not her usual sigh, though. Her nose was high bridged, and her complexion was smooth and free of the moles she was so self-conscious about. Her eyes were big and her irises strong. The curve of her eyebrows was beautiful, without so much as a hair out of place. Her fingers were thin, the tips narrow and shapely. No longer were her breasts uneven; in size, shape, and bounce, they were close to the ideal Chika had envisioned, and her crooked legs were straight and slender now, too. She smiled, spun, and struck a pose. Every move she made was angelic.

Her one complaint would be that her clothes were a bit garish. They were appropriate as a magical-girl costume, but everything about the attire was aggressively unique. Pechka's body was no less distinctive in its impact, but the clothes left too strong an impression for day-to-day wear.

Chika transformed into Pechka and stripped off her clothes and accessories. Then she slipped into a white dress, worthy of a rich lady visiting a summer resort. She'd bought it because she wanted it, even though it didn't suit her, but without the confidence to wear it, she'd left it to rot in her dresser.

Careful not to alert her family, she sneaked out of the house.

It had been a year and a half since she first became a magical girl back in her second year of middle school, but she was in her third year already. Her days of simply gazing at herself in the mirror were over. For so long she'd let helping people take up all her free time, always coming up with some excuse to postpone this day, but she couldn't put it off any longer. Now was the time to act.

She'd had no time to make a nice boxed lunch by hand, so while she was out, she used Pechka's magical ability to create a delicious meal. It appeared a bit boring but tasted delectable. She packed it into a lunch box and quickly wrapped it. With that, her gift was complete.

She walked onto the baseball field. For a year and a half, she'd worried that maybe Pechka wasn't actually pretty, that she was just the same old Chika, and she would get snubbed. But the shock, envy, and jealousy from the other girls blew all her worries away. The whispering sea of fans parted before Pechka. Looks determined your place here, so Pechka took priority over those mascara-covered girls. She strode forward boldly. Somehow, she managed to walk like a model on the runway, something she never could have pulled off as her normal self.

Beyond the sea of fans was Ninomiya himself, chatting and laughing. His friends, upon spotting Pechka, began poking the boy's arm and pointing at her in astonishment. Then he looked at her. She had no idea what his expression was—she couldn't bring herself to meet his eyes. Staring at the tips of his muddy spiked shoes, she quickly blurted, "I'm a big fan. Good luck out there," and shoved the wrapped lunch at him. Ninomiya may have said something, but she didn't hear it—right after throwing the gift at him, she ran away.

Just as they had done upon her arrival, the sea of fans parted, and Pechka headed home. She sneaked past her family to her room, dispelled her transformation, and flopped onto the bed. There she writhed, moaning and groaning unintelligibly.

Her magical phone chirped with the text-alert tune, but she was in no state to check it. One moment she fidgeted atop her bed, and in the next she suddenly hit the ground hard without warning, writhing not in love but in physical pain. Dirt and pebbles filled her mouth, and her nose and forehead stung like they'd been scraped across something. Her soft, clean bed had transformed into a hard and deadly weapon.

She flipped over to try to check what was going on, but a blinding light kept her from opening her eyes. The insides of her eyelids were a searing white. Slowly, she acclimated to the light, until she could finally take in her strange, abnormal surroundings.

The sun was intensely bright—blazing hot and radiant. Patches of weeds dotted a wasteland stretching into the horizon. She could see tall constructs that looked like skyscrapers, three in total, but they were all crumbled. This was when Chika realized something: Her vision had become much, much better than when she was human. Without even realizing it, she had transformed into Pechka.

She patted her hands, feet, upper body, and lower body, examining herself closely. She had definitely transformed into Pechka. As a test, she hopped a little and flew straight up ten feet, then stuck the landing. Yup, she'd definitely transformed—though that had never happened involuntarily before.

"Where am I? Why am I here?"

Where indeed? It didn't resemble anywhere in Japan. She'd heard you could find vast stretches of land like this in Hokkaido, but she doubted they came with broken-down buildings. Maybe she was in some foreign country that was embroiled in civil war or had been invaded by another nation. That would explain the high-rise building, and this desolate landscape would match the blood-soaked circumstances. It would also explain why there were no people.

But why was she here? Pechka didn't understand at all. She'd been on her bed moments earlier, squirming with joy. Maybe she'd just been too happy, so the bad stuff had come for her to balance it out. Or perhaps this was her punishment for using her powers for something other than good deeds.

Oh yeah. Pechka recalled that just before she'd been transferred here, her magical phone had rung. Maybe that had something to do with this.

She took out the little device. Besides the apps of a regular smartphone, it had an amazing portability function that enabled the user to materialize things out of thin air. It was also shaped like a heart—exactly the sort of style appropriate to a magical girl. But such an oddly shaped screen would be unpopular on a normal phone because it was impractical and hard to read.

Displayed on the screen in simple serif typeface were the words Tutorial Mode. Pechka cocked her head in confusion. She'd never seen this before. She tried to start her messaging app, but for some reason, the phone wouldn't respond. The message started to scroll of its own accord.

In this tutorial mode, you will personally experience battle in *Magical Girl Raising Project*. Defeat your enemies to gain magical candy.

Magical Girl Raising Project? *Battling? Enemies? Magical candy?*

Then Pechka noticed the ground rumbling around her—but it wasn't an earthquake. Only a specific section of the ground was moving, not the entire earth—rumbling, swelling, and bursting from within its depths to create a hole. A white arm reached out from it, followed by its owner. Teeth rattling, bones popping, it slowly rose up. Darkness obscured its eye sockets, hiding them from view. But even if she had seen them, there would surely be nothing inside. Altogether, there were five animated skeletons, reminiscent of gods of death. She was surrounded.

Five skeletons have appeared.

The message appeared on her phone's screen. Pechka swallowed the scream rising in her throat and steeled her buckling legs. Gritting her teeth, she held her weapon, a spatula, at the ready. Still confused as to what was going on, she smacked away the skeletal hand reaching for her. She kicked the bony figure that rushed at her, then she drew back again, dodging the skeletons grabbing at her from either side. Then she froze. The first one, the one she'd kicked, was lying facedown on the ground and holding her leg.

The touch of the skeleton's hand was cold and repulsive, bringing her to a halt. Her magical strength normally would have allowed her to easily brush it off and crush it underfoot. But Pechka was at her limits, emotionally speaking, and she was on the verge of panicking. For all her magical enhancements, Pechka's special ability was just food preparation. When it came to fighting, her own body was all she could rely on. She had no other choice but to hit and be hit, kick and be kicked. This wasn't something a middle school girl with an average, peaceful life could handle.

The four other skeletons closed in on her as if in slow motion. But just before they reached her, they were sliced in half from skull to pelvis, clattering to the floor.

"…Huh?!"

At her feet, the skeleton that had been holding her was now cut cleanly into three vertical slices. The deep gouges in the ground from the expert cuts were evidence of how much force had been behind each strike. Flustered, Pechka shook her leg, and the bony fingers clasping her fell off.

What happened? What happened? As far as she could tell, she hadn't awoken to any new power or unlocked something sealed inside her. This wasn't Pechka's handiwork. Looking all around, she spotted a figure beyond the dust storm with her magically enhanced vision. It was too small to be an adult male…

It was a girl. In her right hand dangled a katana. She must have been her rescuer. Over a mile of distance separated the two, but ruined buildings and weeds were the only other things around, and compared with them, the girl seemed a more likely suspect.

That the girl had saved her meant she was friendly—she had to be. To Pechka, who had suddenly been thrown into a confusing landscape and forced to fight terrifying monsters, she was a savior. The rescued girl sprinted over, and in a flash she had covered the mile distance and was vigorously bowing her head. "Thank you very much!"

Pechka gently lifted her head to look at her protector, who really was a girl. She was garbed in samurai-like clothing, but it was dramatically stylized, as was her long ponytail, bound into a unique accessory that resembled a blooming flower at the end. Her garb looked less like a samurai's attire and more like something else—like a magical girl's costume. Not to mention that no one but Pechka's fellows would be capable of attacking an enemy from over a mile away with a katana.

"Are you…a magical girl?" asked Pechka.

No response.

"Um, my name's Pechka. I'm a magical girl, too."

No response. The girl merely stared.

Sensing that this was a sign to hurry, Pechka went on. "I wonder where we are. Would you happen to know? I just randomly ended up here, and I really didn't know what's going on, and then I got scared when those skeletons appeared, and I'm really in a mess."

"Must I do this again? Is it not over?"

"Huh?"

"I don't like it. It's...not right." The girl's eyes were focused on one point, yet she didn't appear to be seeing anything. Her gaze was aimed at Pechka, but she was looking off somewhere else entirely. The girl reached out her hand and wrapped her fingers around Pechka's throat.

Unable to move, Pechka didn't resist, letting her do as she would. The girl's fingers felt cold. Pechka swallowed audibly. The grip around her throat tightened. Muscle and flesh contracted. The katana in the girl's right hand edged slowly closer to her captive's throat. Something was chattering—Pechka's own teeth.

"Is it not over?" the girl murmured. "Come on, Musician."

"I—I don't know anything," stammered Pechka. "I—I don't know what's going on, either. I blinked, and then I was here."

The samurai stared at her with those unseeing eyes. Her grip weakened, and her katana dropped to dangle at her side again. She let go of Pechka's throat and pushed her away. Unable to stand her ground, Pechka fell on her bottom and peered up at the other girl. Her teeth were still chattering, hard.

"It seems you are not the Musician. That person is more...like..." The girl turned her back to Pechka and began to stagger unsteadily away, her dragging katana carving a trail as she went. She was muttering something under her breath, but Pechka couldn't quite hear.

Still sitting on the ground, Pechka watched her go. After all that, she still didn't know where she was or how she ended up there. But she had no urge to go after the other girl.

☆ Magical Daisy

The skeletons had proven surprisingly fragile—about as strong as human bones, perhaps. They broke from Magical Daisy's kicks and shattered under her punches. This sort of violence stirred a visceral disgust within her, but she was what you'd call a veteran. She would have quit long ago if this were enough to break her.

"Daisy Punch!"

It was just a normal punch.

"Daisy Kick!"

It was just a regular kick.

Yet Magical Daisy felt that naming her moves made them stronger, so she'd named her ordinary punches and kicks as if they were special attacks. She believed that there had to be power, or something, in saying it out loud.

"Daisy Beam!"

It was just a normal beam—well, obviously not.

The Daisy Beam was her killer move—and not in the figurative sense. This move was literally guaranteed to kill. In addition to supernaturally enhanced physical strength, girls chosen by the Magical Kingdom were each given a unique magical ability. This was what made them "magical" girls. Daisy's ability was the Daisy Beam. By pointing her finger, she could shoot a light ray around four inches in diameter. It instantly vaporized anything it touched, though she didn't understand how it worked. Palette had explained that it disassembled the target on a molecular level, causing it to quickly disintegrate and disperse into the air. She could, of course, vary the beam. If she spread her hand wide, it would shoot a light ray about a foot and a half in diameter, a much wider attack area.

She had never used this move to kill anyone. It was for eliminating waste and obstacles. She'd once suggested to the Magical Kingdom that it might be helpful to the world to use her beam to clear industrial or atomic waste, but she'd received the notice that magical girls were not permitted to influence trade or industry in the human world. It felt like they'd warned her, *Keep the showboating to a minimum!* as if they'd seen a narcissism in her that she didn't realize she had. This hadn't done her self-esteem any favors.

On a personal level, Daisy considered using the beam on living things to be the deepest of taboos, and the Magical Kingdom and its mascots also heavily restricted its use. But when assaulted by monsters that were clearly not alive—and thanks to the video game–like message Five skeletons have appeared—she'd fired in the moment, without hesitation. One shot of her beam had blown the skeletons away, along with her pent-up stress. But at the same time, it gave her second thoughts. She'd gotten carried away.

"So, uh, where am I?" As usual, she was talking to herself, but she really meant it this time. She'd read that the game had begun, and a second later, she'd been transformed into her magical-girl form and transported into the middle of this wasteland, all alone. Then the skeletons had attacked her.

The land was flat in every direction as far as Magical Daisy could see. She'd never been to Mexico or Africa, but she imagined the sun here was just as hot. She'd probably be suffering some burns if not for her enhanced skin. The only other thing in her field of vision besides the sun and wasteland were some dilapidated buildings. Daisy checked her magical phone. She couldn't access her profile page anymore, and there was a message on her screen. It read:

The tutorial has ended.
You earned 5 magical candies.

Magical candy. That reminded Daisy—the phone had said something about that, right before the skeletons had appeared. She also felt like she'd heard that phrase before somewhere. Where had it been?

Please head to town.

Town? She saw only wasteland around her. But maybe if she traveled higher, she might be able to see around a little more. Daisy dashed over to the high-rise buildings. Up close, she could see the full extent of their dilapidation, their walls stained brown from the dust clouds. The amount of chips, cracks, and general signs of erosion led her to believe that these buildings had been there for a long time, not just a few years. One building was leaning to the side, with everything above the tenth floor entirely crumpled. It was about as tall as the other buildings.

Taking care not to cause the whole thing to collapse, Daisy quickly scaled the building. With her magically enhanced strength, running up the wall was nothing. Upon reaching the top, she surveyed her surroundings. The wind gusted harder up here, so she held her skirt down. Even the sun seemed to be stronger here, possibly because she was closer to it. As she'd expected, though, the view was much clearer. Her left hand to her forehead to block out the light, she looked off into the distance. Her abnormally powerful eyes meant she could see farther than any other living creature.

"Hmm... Is that it?" In the distance, she could see a cluster of buildings. It was the only thing in view that could pass for anything like a town. The rest of the wasteland was dotted with more ruins like the one she was currently standing on. She examined everything around her, checking each and every one of the buildings. They were all exactly the same, right down to the angle of their tilt and the patterns of broken glass in the windows, just like in a video game. One building in particular caught her eye—atop it was a figure.

Daisy jumped back as soon as she caught sight of the figure in the distance. A crack had appeared in the building's roof right under where she'd been standing—and it was no natural fissure. Something extremely sharp had sliced through the concrete like butter. She looked at the faraway shape again. Did the attack come from over there?

They were holding some sort of pole. At this distance, it was too far for even Daisy's superpowered eyes to make out exactly what it was.

Just then, the figure moved, seeming to raise the pole, and the sunlight glittered off it, sparkling. It was metal... A blade? Daisy flung herself to the ground. The edge of the roof fractured, slid, then fell to the ground and shook the earth. Even from way up high, Daisy could see the dust cloud that ensued.

There was no mistaking it: The damage had occurred right after the figure's movement. She thought they might be hurling slices of wind at her, but there was zero delay between the figure's actions and the destruction that followed. It wasn't quite like a projectile.

Still on the ground, Magical Daisy stuck her arms out in front of her, facing the figure, and thought. Daisy had been hit yet had taken no damage. Could it have been a warning, or maybe a ruse? The move had caused her to jump back and drop down, but she wasn't quite sure if she'd still have been unhurt if she hadn't taken defensive action.

If the figure had missed deliberately—and even if it hadn't—it seemed different from those lifeless and mindless skeletons. Regardless of how the figured had attacked, they seemed human-like. And Magical Daisy couldn't use her beam on a human...or any living creature, whatever it was.

After a moment's hesitation, she looked at the giant split in the side of the building and decided she couldn't ignore the enemy anymore. She aimed her outstretched arm a little lower and then shot her Daisy Beam. It scored a direct hit on the base of the build-ing, causing the nearly toppled structure to lean even farther to the side. After one more shot, down came the building in a plume of smoke.

The figure jumped from the collapsing building and landed on the ground. Meanwhile, Daisy jumped from her own vantage point and rushed to close the distance between them. The stranger did the same. Still running, they slashed once, twice, swinging downward and striking upward.

Daisy dodged every attack. The effects were basically the same as if the figure were swinging a katana at close range. The cuts followed the blade's trajectory, so as long as Magical Daisy moved herself out of the way, she could dodge. They were all highly telegraphed.

"Daisy Beam! Daisy Beam! Daisy...Beeeam!"

She unleashed shot after shot, never aiming directly at her opponent. She directed each attack toward the ground, vaporizing the dirt and kicking up dust to block her foe's vision. Then she dashed forward into the thick clouds of dust that billowed in the air.

She could sense a presence. It was sticky and thick, not even trying to hide itself. A strike at her feet slithered along the ground. Back-stepping, she dodged and kicked low, but her attacker was pressed to the ground. Daisy meant to hit their temple with her toes, but instead, she scored a hit on their forehead—or rather, their forehead had blocked her kick. Her foot went numb. The figure then thrust a blade from below, aiming for her throat. Magical Daisy barely dodged, the blade cutting into her shoulder. She was too far away, and her opponent's katana prevented her from getting close.

Daisy dropped down and slid ahead, trying to take out their legs. Once the opponent fell, the two became entangled. The katana was knocked aside as the pair grabbed at each other's arms and legs, each grappling with an unseen enemy.

As she touched her opponent, she understood: This was a magical girl's body, and a toned one, at that. It belonged to someone who, like Daisy, had punished herself in training so that she would be able to fight someone and win.

Daisy grabbed the girl's sleeve and threw her. Just before the girl hit the ground, Daisy felt her legs being swept out from under her, and the pair collapsed in a heap.

"Ha-ha!" Her opponent barked out a laugh. Daisy bit one back.

Daisy struck with her elbows and fists and was paid back in kind with a strike to her knees. As her opponent's arm snaked around her neck, she kicked away to distance herself. *All right, what's she going to do? And what's my next move?* Heat coursed through her entire body. Slowly, the dust cloud faded, and then a sudden gust blew in, wafting the rest of it away. When the debris settled, only Magical Daisy remained.

"...Huh?" Had her opponent run away? Well, if they had, that was the best outcome. But still, Daisy was upset—or maybe just let down. She couldn't deny that she was unsatisfied. She'd enjoyed scuffling blind with a strange opponent, and she was sure they had as well.

"You're not the Musician."

Daisy spun around at a voice, but no one was there. She still had no clue what that fight was about. Most likely, she had faced another magical girl, but she couldn't be sure.

As her body released the intense heat of the fight, her mind cooled as well. Remembering her original objective, she looked toward the town.

Now a cloud of dust had whipped up in front of it. She could see silhouettes, and not just one or two. They moved furiously. There was a lone figure, surrounded by a hoard of white...skeletons. Someone was being forced to battle skeletons, just like Daisy. She reached out with her right hand and was just about to fire a killer Daisy Beam when she realized with a start what she was doing. Her target was quite far away. If she missed, it could be really bad.

"Augh! This sucks! Damn it!" she shouted, and she charged in.

☆ Pechka

The high-rise building was completely empty on the inside. Pechka could see no traces of it having been used as retail space or an office building, and no sign that it had been lived in as an apartment, either. There was truly nothing. There were only floors and rooms with broken glass windows that let the wind blow through.

She searched for clues as to where in the world she could be, but by the third building, she was disheartened. By the fifth building, she was distraught. And on the eighth building, she finally broke down. She was well aware of this, too. Pechka was not a strong-hearted girl. Clearing away the dust on the ground, she sat and leaned against a wall. All that would come out of her was a sigh.

She had no idea where she was. Monsters had attacked her, and the magical girl who had fought them off for her had almost killed her. And to top it off, her magical phone was totally broken.

Her e-mail app wouldn't open, and she couldn't even make calls to notify the outside world of her distress.

Right now, the baffling message Magical candy: 0 was displayed on her screen. What was that? It certainly had a magical-girl ring to it. But she'd never heard the term before.

Pechka thought of Ninomiya. This was just an attempt to escape the real world. She couldn't even be sure this was reality, anyway, so she'd rather be thinking about Ninomiya. Had he eaten the boxed lunch she had given him? The food she created with her magic was really delicious. But maybe it hadn't been to his preference. Despite how reliably good her creations were, not everyone had the same sense of taste. And besides, he might have thrown it out without even trying it. Some people might think it would be dumb of him to eat a boxed lunch he received from some fan he'd never met before, not knowing what was inside. If Pechka were in Ninomiya's shoes, she wouldn't have wanted to eat it.

Oh, this is no use. Even thinking about Ninomiya caused her to spiral into negativity, even though he should have been her greatest source of happiness.

Pechka broke out into tears, sobbing soundlessly. She was worried that if she made any noise, those skeleton-like monsters might attack her again, so she allowed only her tears to come out. The droplets ran down her cheeks to her chin, where they splashed onto the arms that hugged her legs. When she wasn't transformed, plain Chika was a crybaby, but Pechka had never cried once. Still, now she cried and cried and cried until she was exhausted enough to nod off to sleep—until a tremor against her back jolted her awake again.

She opened her eyes and immediately pressed her right ear against the wall. There were footsteps. And the sound of...hooves? And talking. More than one person. There were others in here. Pechka removed her ear from the wall and started to make her way toward the sounds' origin, trying to keep as quiet as possible. Maybe this time she'd meet someone normal. Maybe they'd explain the situation and tell her what to do. Maybe they'd save her.

Of course, it was possible that wouldn't be the case. In fact, it was more than likely. Since Pechka had been brought to this place, she had yet to encounter anyone she could even have a proper conversation with, never mind determine whether they were friendly or not. If these people seemed normal, she'd try to chat with them. Otherwise, she'd run away before they found her. With that in mind, she crept silently toward the source of the footsteps. After every step, she waited thirty seconds before taking another. Sweat ran down her chin now where the tears had been before.

"I *told* you, didn't I?" That was Japanese. The intonation was a little weird in places, but Pechka could understand what the person was saying. At the very least, it seemed like someone she could communicate with. "I told you if we climbed a building, we could get a better view. *Alors*, Rionetta, you said—"

"Are you still cross I made that comment about twits and high places? Feeling miffed about that?"

"Oh, you think *that* made me angry? *Non!*"

"You two, stop fighting," came a third voice.

Pechka carefully peered through the doorway. The room she observed was missing the ceiling, making it the de facto roof. In it stood three figures. Not three people—three figures. Pechka had decided to talk to them if they seemed normal, but she halted right outside.

"This isn't a fight, *non*! It's a legitimate objection!" The girl with the strange intonation seemed fairly ordinary. She was wearing a costume based on a shrine maiden's outfit. Most likely, she was a magical girl just like Pechka. While her distinctly Japanese fashion didn't match her manner of speech, at the very least, she didn't look weird.

"This isn't a fight at all. Fighting is the sort of behavior done among *equals*."

That voice belonged to another individual, one who also appeared as a regular girl, though a little on the large side. Her Lolita fashion, with the bonnet and bloomers and all, might have passed for what a regular hobbyist would wear if it weren't a magical girl's costume. Her face was cute, but it seemed somehow fake. When Pechka noticed the girl's exposed armpits and wrists, her

breath caught in her throat. The girl's skin was textured just like that of a human's, but her joints were all ball joints. It wasn't a human, but a doll. And it was talking.

And the third girl was even more shocking than the doll. She was also lovely, her clothes mostly purple and adorned with feather-like decorations and a big ribbon to add some flair. But then there was her lower half: a horse. Not that she was riding a horse—oh, no. It was as if someone had taken a horse, removed its head, and replaced it with the upper body of a human girl, just like the mythical centaur, or whatever it was called.

Were these figures monsters like the skeletons, or were they magical girls? Pechka couldn't decide, and that meant it was best to avoid them. Slowly, carefully, she began backing away. She had to leave before they noticed her. But after three steps back, their magical phones started ringing. The three girls took out their devices, which indicated to her that they were, in fact, magical girls, but at the same time, Pechka's phone rang. Startled, all three girls turned to her.

Pechka took off without sparing so much as a glance behind her.

☆ Magical Daisy

The maid Daisy had saved introduced herself as Nokko. She was dressed like a traditional maid, her platinum-blond hair tied up on both sides with ribbons, and she even had a mop in hand, decorated with the same ribbon. Age-wise, she appeared about ten years old and stood a head shorter than Daisy.

According to her, she became the magical girl Nokko at age four. At the time, her judgment had been severely underdeveloped, so when creating her magical-girl name, she'd thought they were asking for her real name and so answered cheerfully, "Nokko!" And thus she'd ended up stuck with that name. She had later submitted thirty requests for a name change, but every one was rejected. The Magical Kingdom's ruling was that, once decided, a magical girl's name could not be changed, barring extreme circumstances—even if the name was created by a four-year-old barely capable of making a sound decision.

Nokko seemed embarrassed as she told Daisy the origin of her name. As she related her story, with a mix of self-deprecation and complaint, she repeatedly played with the ribbons in her hair as she spoke. It was adorably innocent.

Daisy asked her, "Do you know where we are? Why we were brought here?"

"I have no idea," Nokko replied. "I was looking at my bank book, and then suddenly, I came here."

Daisy was curious as to why she would be reviewing her transactions in the middle of the night, but that was probably irrelevant. Confirming the date with Nokko, they found they were on the same page time-wise. Each of their incidents had occurred at the same time on the same day.

"Um...," Nokko began.

"Yes?"

"Are you *the* Magical Daisy?"

"Huh? Yeah, I am."

"Wow! You're just like on TV! Were the episodes based on real life?"

"Oh yeah. Some of it was exaggerated, though."

Nokko seemed to be a fan of *Magical Daisy*...or rather, magical girls in general. As her excitement rose, she started squealing. The most common reason anyone joined the ranks of magical girls was that they loved the anime and manga. In that sense, Daisy was the same. Her love had led her to this path herself. So she didn't find it surprising or suspicious that Nokko was a magical-girl fan.

But it made Daisy happy to meet a fan of the show in real life, and it made her even happier to see Nokko so overjoyed. Watching the young girl talk excitedly about what she remembered, the parts that had made her cry, her most hated villains, and the episodes she'd watched with sweaty hands clenched, she thought, *I have to protect her.*

"I was so excited for the reruns every week!" Nokko exclaimed.

"I was still in middle school during the original airing... Just how old was I when the rerun started?"

Was this how pop idols felt about their fans? Though Daisy was more like a retired pop idol now that the anime was over, but seeing Nokko's enthusiasm tugged at her heartstrings and gave her strength.

The two of them chatted excitedly for a while about their memories of *Magical Daisy* until the sound of their magical phones ringing brought them back to reality. They were in a strange, unknown land with skeletal remains scattered all about. On the screen was the message:

Please head to town.

They just never let up! Daisy grumbled in her head, but it looked like they had no choice but to obey. So she told Nokko about the apparent town she'd spotted from atop the building and suggested they head there in hopes that it might shed some light on their situation.

"I'll do my best to not get in the way," Nokko replied, blushing. Seeing her flushed face lifted Daisy's spirits.

It was quite a ways to the town, but with their magical-girl legs, it wasn't too much effort. Based on that battle with the skeletons, Daisy assumed Nokko wasn't much of a runner, or possibly not very confident in her physical abilities, so she refrained from going too fast, but even with that, they covered the twelve-odd miles to their destination in only about ten minutes.

The "town" was just what she'd seen from a distance: a town in name only, with none of the things necessary for an actual settlement. The buildings were in better shape than the dilapidated ones out in the wasteland, but the road showed no signs of maintenance. Clouds of dust floated through the empty streets. From their vantage point on the outside, there was no pedestrian traffic. After Daisy warned Nokko to stay close, they walked in together.

Upon entering the town, they encountered a wide-open area.

It looked like the town square. In the center was an indentation carved out of stone with a mermaid statue sitting in it. It must have once been some kind of fountain, though the water was all dried up. In its place sat piles of sand, which spoke to the length of time it had gone without water. There were two people in the square.

"Whoa, whoa, whoa!" a strange voice shouted. One of the girls, her face red with excitement, pointed their way. "Are you for real? Are you the actual Magical Daisy?"

"Uh, yeah, I guess I am," Daisy replied.

"Wow! You're really the real deal? Cool!"

This had to be another magical girl. She was wearing quite the outlandish outfit: a helmet with a visor and a near-future-style full-body suit that clung to her frame. A gun sat in the holster at her waist, but it looked more like a toy ray gun than a real weapon. The entire costume screamed *Defense force battling to protect Earth from monsters and aliens!* Daisy had always loved to watch summer reruns of that stuff, and while she hadn't grown up during the first airings of those types of shows, it was familiar enough to instill a sense of nostalgia in her.

"Oh, I may not look it," said the girl, "but I'm sorta the nerdy *otaku* type. I watched *Magical Daisy* as it aired, and of course, I collected all the DVD sets, too. Oh, I'm so stoked! So pumped! I can't believe Magical Daisy is real!"

"May not look it"? Please. Everything about her screams "obsessed," thought Daisy. But that aside, it made her honestly happy to see a fan overjoyed.

"Meow-Meow! Meow-Meooow! Come here!" Apparently, the nerdy girl wasn't just imitating a cat. She was calling someone's name.

Cautiously, a girl in a costume resembling a cheongsam dress walked forward, her hair tied up in two buns. She looked like a Chinese stereotype, complete with an accent. "She you friend, Yumenoshima?" It was so cliché. But from her rear was growing a thick, monstrous, reptilian tail, giving her style an unbalanced sort of punch.

"Wait, Meow-Meow," said the first girl, "you don't know who Magical Daisy is? You must live under a rock."

"Oh, she famous? Pardon me, then."

"This isn't something I can pardon you for! This is common knowledge!"

The defense army–esque girl introduced herself as Genopsyko Yumenoshima, and the girl in Chinese fashion as @Meow-Meow. *Those are both crazy names*, Daisy thought, but she kept that to herself so as not to be rude. But…

"Those names are pretty weird," Nokko blurted.

"People say all the time," @Meow-Meow said.

"I was going for a strong impression," Genopsyko added. They both laughed, causing Daisy and Nokko to start giggling, too. Daisy considered scolding Nokko and telling her that it didn't matter what their names were, but the urge dissipated with one look at the younger girl.

Next, Nokko introduced herself and the story behind her name, which only elicited more laughter. Maybe the origin of her name and how she'd tried to change it afterward was just a funny story she told everyone.

The four of them sat in a circle on the lip of the mermaid-statue fountain.

It turned out that Genopsyko and @Meow-Meow were not longtime friends but had met after arriving here, just like Daisy and Nokko. They had experienced much the same thing: They both received a text in the middle of the night, and then suddenly they were in a wasteland, skeletons closing in.

"Oh yeah, and we also meet other magical girls," said @Meow-Meow. "Seems they in same boat." She explained that a group of girls had already passed through town.

"Where did they go?" asked Daisy.

"They finish business here, then go."

"They wouldn't tell us what they were here for," added Genopsyko. "Pretty shady. Magical girls play as dirty as you'd expect."

"I said no good to be separated. But they have own plans, so they leave fast."

According to @Meow-Meow, there had been four magical girls in total: one who looked like a doll, another like a shrine maiden, one with the lower body of a horse, and an unconscious fourth tied to her back with loops of clear string.

"Huh?" said Daisy. "Shouldn't you have done something?"

Genopsyko explained, "They said she was tied up to prevent her from crying, going berserk, or running away and getting into trouble."

"We talk to them, and they no seem like bad people."

Daisy was in no position to worry about others, but this still concerned her. There was no guarantee their strange circumstances wouldn't cause someone to panic and end up hurting another... She'd nearly done the same earlier.

"They said there more magical girls here," said @Meow-Meow.

"Apparently, they also came here, finished their business, and left, but I have no idea what's going on... Huh?" Before Genopsyko could finish her sentence, she froze, mouth still agape. She stared at the screen of the device in her right hand, the light reflecting off her visor. "We got a message! Everyone, hurry up and turn on your phones!"

The message that had been on the screen before, Please head to town, was gone. Now their phones read Support commands added.

"Support commands?" Daisy wondered. The word Support was clickable. She tapped it with her fingertip.

MASTER SIDE #1

The classroom was wreathed in flames.

The ancient wooden building didn't have any fire sprinklers installed, as it should have, and there was more than enough fuel. Fire spread from desks to chairs, bookcases to wallpaper, as window frames and glass melted and ran in the heat. The red of the flames illuminated everything, poisonous black smoke filling the air.

In the middle of it all stood two girls, their presence clashing with the hellish scene. They stared each other down.

One girl was red. Her hair was crimson, her dress the same color as the flames, and her expression one of blazing rage and passion, distorting her fundamentally statuesque face into something beastly. The girl held both fists in front of her, lightly clenched, crouching and ready in a low stance.

The other girl was white. She wore a snowy sailor blouse and skirt, resembling a school uniform, and an old cloth bag hung from her waist. Her hands held a *naginata*-like pole arm at the ready. In contrast to the all-out fury surrounding the red girl, the white girl's face was completely impassive.

The red girl moved first. Crouching even deeper into her low stance, she appeared to glide across the ground as she stepped forward to kick low from just outside the *naginata*'s range. The strike was probably a feint, a fake, or a distraction. The white girl blocked it with the handle of her weapon as if she'd known exactly what was coming.

The red girl followed up with a second, then a third strike, but she couldn't even break into the weapon's range. On her fourth strike, the *naginata* grazed her, cutting open her foot, which spurted out blood. The red girl let out a sharp cry and then spewed flame from her mouth. This attack was supposed to have shocked the white girl, but she remained emotionless as she spun her blade, extinguishing the human-sized fireball in one swing. Her thin, feminine arms easily wielded the three-foot-long, heavy-looking pole arm like it was a part of her body.

The red girl shouted something and threw herself backward into the flames, then disappeared. A moment later, the fire behind the white girl grew, transforming into the red girl. But the second before she could unleash a devastating roundhouse kick to the back of her opponent's defenseless head, the white girl ducked without so much as a glance—as if she knew exactly what was coming. A whiplike *crack* echoed as the fiery girl's leg tore through empty air. The red girl quickly withdrew into the flames, as if melting into them.

The white girl's expression hadn't changed once since the fight's beginning. Holding the blade in one hand, she flipped it around and then stabbed it into the classroom floor. She reached inside the bag hanging from her waist and removed an object. The light of the flames illuminated the gray body of a commercial fire extinguisher, an object much larger than the bag she'd produced it from. She removed the pin and aimed the nozzle at the flames spreading across the ceiling—at about a forty-five degree angle right above the teacher's desk—and unleashed the coolant fluid.

Something fell from the ceiling, screaming silently, holding its head as it writhed in agony. That *something* was the crimson girl.

Her red clothes, her fiery hair—everything was covered in white foam. Saliva and tears streamed down her face while she writhed in pain.

The white girl calmly approached, raised the big fire extinguisher, and then struck her opponent with it. Five more times she pummeled her, until the red girl moved no more. The victor tossed the fire extinguisher to the side and looked down at her foe. The white girl's expression was just as it had been the moment the battle ended—blank.

The video ended there.

She moved the cursor, closing the video player and browser with a few clicks, then shut down the computer. With the computer off, the one source of light in the room was gone, leaving only darkness, the smell of mold, and the voices.

"And so the villain was apprehended... Man, Snow White's sooo cool," came a satisfied-sounding female voice. She sounded like she was in her midteens. "Flame Flamey was a real powerful fighter, too, but up against Snow White, she was like a liiittle kid. The way Snow White moved, it was like she knew exaaactly where that girl was going! *Nghhh!*" The noise resembled a sob, but her voice was full of joy. "She's reeeally cool! She's totally merciless about hunting evil magical girls! Flamey deserved that for manipulating them into killing each other based on her twisted belief that only the strong deserve those powers! Snow White is strong, kind, and righteous! Hiyah! Hah!"

There was the sound of something clattering to the floor. "But, like, don't you think it's weird to require magical girls to be strong?" the girl went on. "Magical girls are supposed to, y'know, be kind and lovely, and care about things like compassion, friendship, and sincerity and stuff like that!"

"Yes. Perhaps, pon. Nothing wrong with being strong, though." The voice that replied to the girl was high-pitched and childlike, yet its tone was flat and calm.

"I know, right? My teacher said the same thing! Strength isn't all that makes you a magical girl. We don't need people who just want power. It's unacceptable for them to be inciting battle royals, and we can't have magical girls chosen by those deadly competitions, either." She spoke feverishly.

"That's why I'm gonna help Snow White!" she concluded.

CHAPTER 2
GOOD FOOD MAKES EVERYONE HAPPY

☆ **Magical Daisy**

A flourish of trumpets rang out from Genopsyko's magical phone as its screen glowed with all the colors of the rainbow. She dropped the phone, and it skittered across the base of the fountain to smack into the mermaid statue, where it stopped, screen side up. A band of light expanded out of the screen and condensed to form an image: a symmetrical spheroid, its right half black, the left half white. It floated lightly in the air, a butterfly-like wing sprouting from one side. The translucent orb hovered there, illuminating the billowing cloud of sand with its light. It was a hologram.

"Hello, good day, and good evening to all you magical girls! This is Fal, appointed mascot of *Magical Girl Raising Project*, pon!" The high-pitched, synthetic voice was childlike, and yet mysteriously sickening. Daisy's expression soured. Genopsyko, @Meow-Meow, and Nokko all watched her.

Fighting the urge to throw up, Daisy addressed the hologram that had introduced itself as Fal. "What is this? What is going on?"

"*Magical Girl Raising Project* is a next-gen social network game used as a training simulator for magical girls on active duty, and also for testing candidates, pon. The experience you gain here in this virtual space will be directly relayed to your physical bodies, pon. You were all selected through impartial lottery to be test players, pon."

"Virtual space? This isn't the real world?" asked Daisy.

"Exactly! The Magical Trace System–based controls feel just like reality! Plus, there's the gorgeous, hyperrealistic graphics. Those are the two big draws of *Magical Girl Raising Project*, pon."

"Is this really a game?"

"It is, pon. Fal wouldn't lie, pon."

"It's not magic?"

"It's a game created by magic, pon."

Magical Daisy tried to act calm, but inside, she was shaken. Though Fal had explicitly claimed that this was a game, everything seemed so real, despite the strangeness of the scenery. The smell of dust and mold in the dilapidated buildings, the unrelenting sunlight, the sensation of impact when she'd hit the skeletons, the solid feeling of the ground she was standing on—it all screamed "real." But only in a game could skeletons rise from the ground, and only in a game could there exist an endless desert dotted with identical crumbling buildings standing at uniform intervals.

"I didn't hear anything about this!" yelled Genopsyko. "No one even asked if I wanted to participate! Don't you dare give me that, you furry creep!"

"This sort of causes problems for us...," said Nokko. The two of them drew closer to the magical phone. Unfortunately, they were still speaking to a hologram, so they couldn't even grab it by the collar. Not that it had a collar to grab.

But their anger was understandable. You couldn't just spirit someone away without their consent, force them to fight skeletons, then order them to find some town and expect them to accept all of it without grumbling.

"Now, now. Please calm down and listen, pon." Despite the advancing hostility, the mascot, as it had introduced himself, was calm. Its expression hadn't changed—rather, there had been none to begin with.

Daisy's old partner, Palette, had been a small, boisterous fairy with a wide range of emotions.

They're so different, even though they're both mascots, thought Daisy.

"Time is compressed here, so this won't cause difficulty in your day-to-day lives," said Fal. "At this point, we'd like you to spend three straight days participating in the game. But that will only be a moment in the real world, pon. You might have already realized this, but you can all use your magic here, just like in reality, pon. And none of this is dangerous in the least, pon. There are no healing spells, extra lives, or save points, so if you get a game over, you're done, but there will be no damage to your real body, so it's completely safe, pon."

"I get how it works," said Daisy, "but why were we forced to participate? We weren't even asked."

"Well, I'm sure you're all familiar with how unreasonable the Magical Kingdom can be, pon. Or perhaps the reason is that magic itself is the embodiment of irrationality. It's possible that nonconsenting participation is the trigger or key or something, pon."

Whether it knew their thoughts on the matter or not, Fal continued. "Ultimately, this is an official test from the Magical Kingdom, so there's absolutely nothing to worry about, pon. The rewards for completion are *very* generous, and even the participation awards are pretty great. If you can be our test players and help us figure out the bugs, future candidates will owe you a great debt, pon. This game is still a secret, though, so talking about it to anyone but your fellow players is forbidden, pon… But keeping secrets is part and parcel of being a magical girl, so it'll be easy for you, pon. And so, will you participate, pon? Everyone else has already started, pon."

Fal was looking at Magical Daisy. Genopsyko, @Meow-Meow,

and Nokko all had their eyes on her, too. Daisy glanced at Nokko, feeling she had to keep her safe.

☆ **Pechka**

Pechka was still confused, but she was locked into playing the game. She personally had a ton of things she'd rather do than train or pave the way for future candidates, and she didn't find the reasons she'd been brought to this game in the first place to be particularly convincing. She wanted to apologize and bow out, but the other three had different plans.

"I don't appreciate such forceful measures," said the doll girl, "but if it's the Magical Kingdom's work, then I suppose there's nothing to be done. It seems interesting, at least, so I shall accept."

"It would be *magnifique* if this reward is real!" enthused the shrine maiden.

"Yeah," the half-animal one agreed.

"The reward does sound quite splendid," agreed the doll girl, "but this doesn't really feel like something the Magical Kingdom would do."

"But it's so *fantastique*! With ten billion yen cash, you could live the magical-girl *vie luxe!*"

"What a narrow-minded plan for your life."

With the others like this, Pechka didn't want to be the only one to stand up and say she wouldn't participate. Just like any other plain, introverted middle school girl, she was good at reading the social situation. So she laughed a little and nodded, a vague smile on her lips.

"Now then," said Fal, "you need to form a party, pon. You can have up to four people, pon. Forming a party will allow you to use items that afford all kinds of benefits, pon. Once you install the map app, it will display the locations of your members, and you only need to carry one copy of the items you use as a party, pon."

The four of them exchanged looks, and after a few moments, all eyes ended up on Pechka. Somehow or other, she knew what was on their minds. They were likely thinking, *I don't wanna party up with a weak-looking, clearly useless chicken.*

"If you don't mind, would it be possible for you to tell us your magical ability?" the doll girl asked her.

"Yeah, I am *très curieuse* about that."

They weren't just thinking she was no good. They'd gone and said it.

"Uh, I can make delicious food...if I have just five minutes..."

The other girls exchanged looks. Pechka knew what that meant, and it hurt. She could sense the silent messages passing between them, right over her head: *What do we do with* that? *She's clearly useless. Maybe we should just leave her here.*

"Err...it is possible to change party members during the game, pon. You can add, drop, and swap to suit the situation, pon."

The three girls' eyes locked. The centaur girl nodded. And that was how the four of them became a party. Pechka was fed up with how obviously they were flaunting their opinions.

Two hours passed. In the end, the three girls treated Pechka like any classroom outcast. She was just an extra body to be tossed aside once an actually useful magical girl came along. She sat on the sidelines like a child exempt from gym class as they battled the skeletons. Neither her cooking magic nor her cowardly personality were made for fighting.

The magical shrine maiden was named Nonako Miyokata. The yin-yang ornaments in her hair, deep-slitted red *hakama* pants, and ancient Japanese-style name made her motif obvious, but something about her personality clashed with her pure Japanese aesthetic. It was a little fishy.

"Girls *magiques* are cool! Cute! Strong! This is common knowledge, in my country." From the words she used and her intonation, the sort you'd never hear from a native speaker, Pechka guessed she was a foreigner, perhaps one attempting to be more Japanese than even a native.

She'd proudly told them of her ability to control familiars, but her ability was limited to living creatures. Unable to befriend the skeletons, she kicked and punched them instead.

The doll girl's name was Rionetta. She wasn't like a doll, or resembling a doll—she actually *was* a doll. Her long ribbons dancing in the wind, the ends of her skirt flipping about, her bonnet fluttering with every move as she fought, she seemed to be the picture of a Lolita warrior. But upon closer observation, Pechka could tell that her movements, joints, and expressions were all fake.

She and Nonako Miyokata seemed to be on bad terms and would often butt heads. Her manner of speech was generally refined, but she had a sharp tongue. She was full of jabs and sarcasm. Pechka didn't like her type.

Her magical ability gave her control over dolls, but none of those were around, so she was always in hand-to-hand combat, just like Nonako Miyokata. Her ball joints allowed her to attack at angles impossible for a human, striking sharp and deep from her opponents' blind spots…though whether skeletons had blind spots at all was a mystery.

The centaur girl was named Clantail. She wasn't exactly a centaur, though—more accurately, she could replace her lower body with that of any beast. She'd transform into an alligator and smash the skeletons with her tail, or turn into a horse and grind them to dust with her hooves, choosing the best form for any given situation. Most often, she would revert to a pony, deer, or some other kind of relatively small four-legged animal.

Clantail was also a lot kinder than Pechka had first assumed. It had barely been a day since they'd met in the game, but Clantail had clearly settled in as leader of the three. Watching her break up all of Nonako Miyokata and Rionetta's disputes, Pechka thought, *That looks tough.* Clantail never complained and rarely spoke at all, which added to such an impression.

The three girls fought with some space between them so as not to get in one another's way, striking down skeleton after skeleton. Muscles straining, hair dancing in the wind, white skin flashing from beneath their costumes, there was an ephemerality to them, as if they would disappear if someone touched them. Yet there was also a sensuality within them that made you want to do it anyway. Just watching was enough to make Pechka sigh. Their faces were diverse, but they were all perfectly arranged, with perfect features.

Pechka hugged her legs tighter. What she had wanted more than anything was the beauty of a magical girl. She'd believed that if she could be cute and beautiful, her world would change. She could even give Ninomiya a homemade lunch. And Chika really had changed after becoming a magical girl. Where before, she'd been intensely introverted, now, when she was Pechka—and even when she wasn't—she had been able to act more assertively. But that boldness was born from a sense of superiority and the belief that she was beautiful and special.

But here, she was just another magical girl. Among these others, her looks were average. With her ego popped, all the assertiveness had spilled out of her. Who she was at the core hadn't changed at all. She felt like she'd returned to being the girl who hid in the corner of her middle school classroom. Without anything to hold her up, all that was left was her timid nature. She couldn't fight or object to participating in the game and merely sat in a sort of limbo, watching as the others fought.

While Pechka had been busy picking at her own flaws, tormenting herself over her powerlessness, and otherwise generally moping, the fight had ended. The many dozens of skeleton bodies burst into white dust and faded into the wind.

"It seems my hunch was correct. There are lots of skeletons *ici*."

"Are you trying to take the credit?" demanded Rionetta.

"Ha-ha-ha-ha! Credit certainly doesn't go to *la personne* who couldn't think of it."

"How much candy do we have?" Clantail's interruption brought their argument to a temporary halt. Nonako and Rionetta took out their phones to check.

"*J'ai* seventeen."

"I've got fifteen."

"And I have twenty-eight. How about you, Pechka?" Clantail asked her.

They all turned to her, and Pechka instinctively shrank back.

Nearly dropping her phone as she took it out, she somehow managed to bring up the status screen. "Still zero..." The number displaying the magical candy in her possession hadn't changed.

"I wonder what this means?" asked Nonako.

"It would seem that we do receive candy for defeating monsters," said Rionetta, "but there's quite a lot of variation in amount. Apparently, we don't all receive the same amount for being in a party."

At the bottom of the status screen for the party were three names: Clantail, Nonako Miyokata, and Rionetta.

Clantail seemed to be thinking. "Maybe only the person who strikes the finishing blow receives the candy."

"Yeah, it looks that way from the numbers, *t'sais*?"

"So she who doesn't work shall not eat, then?" Rionetta glanced at Pechka, and she shrank back again.

Clantail put a hand to her chin and pondered some more. "The phones have a transfer function. We should redistribute the candy after each battle."

"Whatever for?" Rionetta protested. "Those who work should get more, should they not? That gives value to the work. Marxism is a relic of the past."

"Maybe that's best when we're fighting hordes of small fry like these," said Clantail. "But when there's fewer enemies, nobody will benefit if we fight among ourselves over the kill."

Rionetta scowled. Pechka could understand Clantail's logic. In RPGs, when big, strong enemies appeared, they would either be solo or in a small party. If they fought over who would strike the finishing blow, the strength of the enemy could turn it into more than a mere hassle.

"*Mademoiselle* Greedy just needs to watch herself."

"You be silent."

"Um...I was just...watching, so I don't need..." Pechka trailed off.

"In that case, fight next time," said Clantail.

Pechka shrank back even farther. She wished she could just disappear.

Fal had told them that for now, they would be logged in to the game for three days in game time, one moment in the real world. Then they would spend three days in real-world time before logging in again. This cycle would continue until someone completed the game. In other words, their situation would continue for at least three days. A dull ache settled in Pechka's stomach.

"Rionetta, are you fine with this?" asked Clantail.

Rionetta seemed quite reluctant, but she nodded. "Good grief. I'm not going to be saving up any candy like this. I need to find a hunting ground."

A hunting ground. That wasn't a phrase you heard every day. Pechka assumed she was talking about a place where monsters spawned or something. A beep came from Rionetta's magical phone as the image of a black-and-white sphere rose from its screen. She must have pressed the HELP button.

"Is something the matter, pon?" Fal asked.

"Do these monsters respawn?" Rionetta asked. "It's a pain to go looking for a new hunting ground."

"The monsters will respawn every morning, pon."

"I see. Another question, then. How much candy must we save until the next level? Isn't that typically something one sees in RPGs?"

"Level?" Fal's expression was as blank as always, but the tone communicated the message clearly. The creature seemed to be thinking, *Why are you asking me that?* "There are no levels in this game, pon."

"Huh?"

"Candy is an item you use at the shop, pon. It is the currency of this world, pon. Well, you may need it for things besides the shop, but for now it's meant for the shop, pon. Oh, and using real money is strictly forbidden, pon."

"A shop? I don't see..."

"Huh? It's in the middle of town. You haven't noticed it, pon?"

Pechka, Nonako, Rionetta, and Clantail all exchanged glances.

"There are lots of useful items for sale," Fal explained, "so do please be sure to use it, pon. Oh, and the grasslands area is now unlocked. Feel free to progress forward, pon."

"An area has been unlocked? Whatever does that mean?" asked Rionetta.

"It means other players have completed the quest needed to unlock the gate to the next area, pon. But there are still rewards for those quests, so you should definitely try to complete them—" Fal's voice cut out. Rionetta had closed the HELP menu.

So the other players were making progress. They, on the other hand, hadn't even figured out that there was a shop in town or that magical candy was the accepted currency there. Never mind Pechka and her reluctance—now the other three were seeming anxious, too.

"For now, let's go back to town. We'll check the location of that shop and then head for the grasslands," Clantail said, and they all nodded.

☆ Shadow Gale

The nurse in black, Shadow Gale, twirled the wrench in her right hand and the scissors in her left before dropping them both into the holsters at her waist. She couldn't help but laugh at herself for doing something so cliché, even in such a strange situation. She put a hand to her chin to wipe away the sweat, but there wasn't any.

The battle has ended.

The physical abilities of magical girls surpassed those of any other living thing. Those who couldn't use their magic in battle, like Shadow Gale, were still capable of putting up a good fight. But she'd still never had any opportunities to use her enhanced physical abilities in real life, so it was shocking to her that just now, she had been able to fight without freezing up or even trembling. Shadow Gale knew better than anyone that she had no real fighting experience. Perhaps it was only the monstrosity of her enemies that enabled her to smash and slice them without mercy. Strange red human bones lay all around her.

"In the end, skeletons are just skeletons... A new color doesn't make them any stronger. They're no worthy foes for the super-heroine Masked Wonder," a masked magical girl murmured with her right arm raised, left arm bent in front of her chest, and legs braced wide in a victory pose.

Shadow Gale had accompanied Masked Wonder since they'd first met at the start of the game, but she still didn't know what those victory poses of hers meant. "Um...are you all right?" she asked worriedly. There was a big bump on the back of Masked Wonder's head as she posed crisply. It glowed bright red and looked terribly painful.

"The Masked Wonder would never fall to such measly wounds! ...It does kinda hurt, though."

"But I never saw anything hit you. Do you know how you got that bump?" The question came from a girl in a wheelchair—but her expression didn't seem concerned at all. The girl's head and arms were covered in so many bandages, it begged the question of what had happened to *her*.

"I was throwing a rock at one of the skeletons when one hit me like *bam*! I didn't think any of them were behind me, though..."

"That may be due to some special ability. We should consider purchasing the monster encyclopedia in the grasslands shop, though it's quite expensive. We should have the funds soon with these monsters around," the girl in the wheelchair said, and then she urged them to check their phones.

When Shadow Gale took out her phone, she saw she had fifty-six pieces.

"Eighty-seven?!" Masked Wonder shouted with surprise. Some-how, despite (possibly) handicapping herself by striking a pose after every downed enemy, she'd defeated more than Shadow Gale. "This should be enough to buy a whole lot at the shop!"

"Wow," said Shadow Gale. "That's way more than the white ones give, isn't it?"

"And this is only after shifting from the wasteland to the grasslands. The enemies here aren't even that much stronger. We're definitely going to have to prioritize opening up new areas," Pfle, the girl in the wheelchair, muttered as if to herself and then nodded. "Bring out the map. We're going back to the grasslands town." She set off on her wheelchair, not even bothering to say *"Follow me"* or *"Let's go together."* Shadow Gale and Masked Wonder hurried to catch up.

Pfle was strong-willed. She hadn't changed one bit since she and Shadow Gale had paired up in the real world. She was the kind of self-centered person who believed her own ideas would benefit others, so naturally, they should obey her. She was arrogant and did whatever she wanted.

And wherever Kanoe Hitokouji was, you'd find Mamori Totoyama. That was still true even now that they were magical girls. Ever since Mamori Totoyama had become Shadow Gale and Kanoe Hitokouji had become Pfle, Shadow Gale had continued to follow the girl and guard her back.

But Mamori would swear on her honor that she did *not* respect, love, or depend on her.

Kanoe took it for granted that she was above everyone else, toyed sadistically with her prey before finishing it, and thought anyone outside of her own family was no better than cattle, slaves, protozoa, or algae. In spite of this, she sincerely believed herself to be graceful, kind, and deserving of others' love. And in her mind, others did love her.

Mamori was closer to Kanoe than anyone else, and even she thought, *Wow, she's such a jerk.* Mamori was sick of it. But even so, she had to stick by Kanoe's side.

The Hitokouji family was a long and unbroken lineage of the ultrarich. For generations, they had amassed, consumed, fattened, and bloated themselves like a clan of monsters. They'd spent more money on their rock garden than the average office worker made in a lifetime. Their mansion was the size of an entire town, and so the area as a whole was named Hitokouji. Even the train stations and bus stops were labeled HITOKOUJI ESTATE. Once, a naughty kid had thrown a rock at Kanoe. The next day, his family had moved far, far away.

And the Totoyama family had served the Hitokoujis for generations. Mamori's parents had even told her that they'd named her Mamori, meaning "protection" in Japanese, so as to ensure she would be able to protect the young mistress. Her very existence was defined by this, and she'd stood behind Kanoe as her servant since before she could remember. If Mamori kicked up a fuss, the adults would get angry at her.

Standing behind Kanoe, Mamori was forced to hear all the praise aimed at her charge. About 60 percent of this was flattery and sycophancy from people attempting to curry favor with the Hitokouji family, while about 40 percent was legitimate. Even among her peers at the rich girls' school she attended, Kanoe dominated both academically and athletically. However, she bored easily, so she never stuck with one sport for long. The proportions of her body were nearly perfect, and her looks were so eye-catching, eight out of ten people would turn around to stare. And through kindergarten, elementary school, middle school, and high school, Kanoe had been the center of everything.

This had made Mamori uncooperative and rebellious at times. But she'd been instructed from a very young age that it was natural for her to serve the Hitokouji family. As she learned more about the world, her view of her parents and herself had become quite cynical.

None of this changed when they became magical girls. Pfle would give orders and Shadow Gale would obey with a tired sigh and a muffled "Yeah, yeah."

Upon getting sucked into the game, Pfle's first order was for Shadow Gale to wrap bandages around her. As Shadow Gale's costume motif was a nurse's outfit, she did carry bandages on her person.

"There are two sorts of magical girls: those who fight and those who don't," said Pfle, looking like she'd been severely injured, even though she wasn't hurt at all. Obviously, the wheelchair, a part of her magical-girl motif, helped in this role. "Those who fight are suited to dirty work. I want people like that near me in case anything happens, since neither of us has the skills for violence."

"So what does that have to do with the bandages?" asked Shadow Gale.

"These girls have an instinctual need to protect the weak. So naturally, they'll feel empathy for the injured, sick, children, elderly, and pregnant women."

Shadow Gale had been completely confused when the skeletons attacked, but Pfle, in comparison, had apparently already considered their future needs. Maybe that was just because defeating monsters, collecting items, and heading to town was such basic RPG fare. Pfle had been using her magic phone earlier, and she'd investigated a lot back at those broken-down buildings, so maybe there had been some hint back there.

Wasn't this a game? Assuming it was, that meant there were other players here, too, right? And if so, then wouldn't they also be magical girls? So wouldn't that suggest the other players weren't opponents to fight? Most likely, that was why Pfle had wanted to be wrapped in bandages and play injured. She was hoping to lure in the magical girls who would fight for such lofty ideals as protecting the weak.

But this was just Shadow Gale's post hoc analysis of events. Pfle wasn't the considerate type who explained her ideas and actions in thorough detail. The theory was largely guesswork, but it was based on years of knowing the girl and understanding her total willingness to take advantage of others' goodwill.

And her plan had already landed one sucker.

Masked Wonder looked like she jumped straight out of an American superhero comic, from her skintight suit and purple cape to the black mask that revealed only her blue eyes and golden hair sparkling in the sun. Her boisterous voice, voluptuous body, and most of all, her penchant for flashy entrances screamed "American," too.

"I am the avatar of justice, here to punish evil! Be you friend or foe?!"

Shadow Gale had been pushing Pfle's wheelchair, as ordered, when they heard the shout from atop a building. Looking up, they saw someone jump down and land, knees bent and raising dust from the impact. Then she lifted her right arm, bent her left across her chest, braced her legs wide, and shouted, "I am the Masked Wonder! A magical girl, the embodiment of justice!"

Shadow Gale didn't even realize it had been a self-introduction until Pfle greeted Masked Wonder in return as if it were nothing at all. "I'm Pfle, and this is Shadow Gale. It's good to meet you, Masked Wonder."

"You seem to be hurt," said Masked Wonder. "Did the skeletons get you?"

"Is that why you called out to us? My, how kind. Thank you very much."

"No need to thank me. A superheroine always helps people in need." Masked Wonder, with her natural urge to offer aid, had come forth to provide her protection, fulfilling Pfle's first objective.

The world just makes things so easy for the evil, mused Shadow Gale.

Later, once they made it to the town, they formed a party, completed the quest, unlocked the gate to the next area, and progressed to the grasslands. There, thanks to Pfle, they managed to quickly complete the quite possibly deliberately obnoxious quest of exploring the vast grasslands from corner to corner. As became apparent, Pfle's power lay in her magical wheelchair. Thanks to it, she could travel fast enough to create shock waves and sonic booms. This cut down massively on the time they needed for the exploration quest, allowing her to complete in only twenty minutes a journey that would have normally taken hours.

While Pfle was busy doing that, Shadow Gale and Masked Wonder had traversed the wasteland to grind some magical candy. Shadow Gale could only speculate as to what Masked Wonder might think, seeing the supposedly injured Pfle rocket away, leaving only a cloud of dust in her wake.

"Wonderful to see her with so much energy," Masked Wonder simply commented. Apparently, she saw it as a good thing.

☆ Magical Daisy

Magical candy functioned as currency in this game, and it was obtained by defeating monsters. In other words, this reward was the whole point of going out to try to beat monsters. So for now, if nothing else, they should be trying to collect more candy, because that was guaranteed to be useful to them. That was how Fal had explained it.

Nokko had echoed Daisy's feeling that the term "magical candy" sounded familiar. When they asked Fal about that, too, Fal had replied, "It's from another testing ground, pon. During that test, magical girls would receive candy by performing their duties to help people. They'd receive more or less depending on the scale of the deed and the amount of gratitude felt. Basically, it was a measurement of their efforts. A numerical representation of their good deeds, pon."

Fal went on to tell them that it had been a robotic, calculating system, devoid of any feelings or community spirit, and it was only thanks to the vehement opposition of certain influential figures that it had been rejected in the testing phase. Only the name was back in its new incarnation.

After that explanation, Magical Daisy thought the story did sound familiar.

The shop in town was empty, just like the rest of the game world. All that was displayed within was a menu listing various recovery items and rations. Daisy pressed the HELP button to call for Fal. "What is this special pass?" she asked. "It says they're selling it for five magical candies."

"You'll need that to cross into other areas, pon," Fal told them. "You only need one per party, pon. The effects of one pass last until morning the next day, pon."

"So I'll buy one, then… Everyone okay with that?" The other

three nodded, and Daisy pointed at the menu. "All right, one pass and...rations?"

"Hunger levels are one of the hidden parameters in this game, pon. Even magical girls need to eat, pon. So please, be sure to eat enough not to starve, pon."

That reminded her how hungry she was. It must have been hours since she'd first entered the game realm. The lack of a clock and the unnatural, unchanging temperature threw off her sense of time.

"And what is this *R*?" Daisy asked. Most of the items had prosaic names, such as Great Recovery Potion, Small Recovery Potion, or Ration—names that made it obvious from a glance what the item's effects were. But among them was an anomaly simply labeled *R*. The mysterious name wasn't the only oddity—it was way more expensive than all the other items. The rations were one candy each, and the great recovery potions were twenty, but this item cost one hundred candy.

"Selecting this will grant you a random item, pon. You could even get a crazy rare item, pon."

"Oh!" Someone made a funny squeal. Daisy looked over to see it was Genopsyko. "I knew it. In games like this, you've gotta have a random element!"

"That something to be so happy about?" asked @Meow-Meow.

"Just imagine!" Genopsyko gushed. "Rolling the dice over and over, never getting the item you want, and before you know it, you're living the dream: debt! And then soon enough, the collectors are even calling your workplace..."

"That no sound good at all."

"You just don't get it, do you? That's what makes it so great! Oh, my collector's soul is on fire!"

"But...we don't have enough candy," said Nokko. And she was right—they didn't have nearly enough. All four of them together had a total of twenty candies, eighty short of purchasing *R*.

"Hmm, that's too bad," said Genopsyko. "But this sort of thing is what makes games so fun."

"There's currently a grand opening sale, pon. The first roll is only ten pieces, pon."

Daisy could swear she saw a glimmer beneath Genopsyko's dark visor. "Let's do it! Let's do it! We gotta do it! C'mon do it, do it now!"

"But it better to buy potion and ration, yes?" said @Meow-Meow.

"We can just buy it with what we have left! It's ninety percent off! We're clearly gonna lose out if we don't do this now!"

Eventually succumbing to Genopsyko's insistence, they bought one *R* and ended up rolling a map. This was an application that modified a magical phone's map to display the area's towns, its owner's current location, and even party member locations if you registered them. Genopsyko proudly puffed out her chest and said, "See? We got a useful item. Good thing we took the gamble, right?"

@Meow-Meow offered the cautious suggestion that they gather more information. Genopsyko boldly exclaimed that she wanted to explore the new area. And Nokko would blindly follow anything Daisy said. Ultimately, Magical Daisy concluded that they should check out the grasslands.

Now that it was settled that they were all participating, Daisy had somehow ended up as the acting leader of their group. She didn't mind having people rely on her, but it'd been a while since people had depended on her. Perhaps she was more excited about this than she had initially realized. She felt they should be careful as they progressed, but there was no guarantee that staying in the wasteland would be beneficial to them. Now that Magical Daisy was in this game and leading a party, she'd like to win, if they could, which meant they needed to catch up to the others who had come by earlier.

Along the road, they fended off sporadic skeleton attacks, using the map in their phones to progress. Eventually, they found their way blocked by an ancient wooden gate, similar in construction to an Edo-period-style checkpoint, sitting between steep peaks. Once they passed through, the wasteland transformed into grasslands. Ankle-high grass rustled and swayed in the wind. The bright field of green stretched out all the way to the horizon, much easier on the eyes than the endless buildings and dirt of the wasteland. The sunshine seemed considerably gentler, too. They were no longer burning up.

"I guess vast open spaces is the common theme." Genopsyko bent forward, put a hand to her visor, and surveyed the land around them. It was all flat, save for the gate behind her. This area had a more pleasant view, but it could get boring, too, if they were stuck there for a long time.

"I wonder if there's another town like before..." Nokko brought up the map on her magical phone.

"A town would be nice, but in games like this, what we *really* need is a spot to farm candy." Genopsyko threw out a couple of quick jabs, as if she was shadowboxing.

"They say we have to complete quest for area gate to open. What we do about that? Fal say quest give candy, too." @Meow-Meow bent down, seemingly observing the grass.

They were all good ideas, which gave Daisy pause. A place to farm was important. Magical Daisy had essentially banned herself from any violence, so the skeletons were the perfect target to unleash her pent-up frustrations on, even if they were pretty weak enemies. The nice part about games was that you could use lethal force with no ethical repercussions.

The main quest was important, too. They'd need to progress into more areas in order to fight stronger enemies, and of course, to complete the game first, they needed to progress the fastest. That was generally how things worked in video games. Thus, the question Daisy asked herself boiled down to whether they should fight or not.

Fighting's fun, after all... In a game, you didn't have to feel any reservations about doing things that would otherwise be taboo. And she wanted to do those things.

"All right, let's head for the town first," said Daisy. "If we go there, we might be able to dig up some information or hints on the area quest, or even something about a good place to farm."

As they progressed through new areas, the parts they'd already covered appeared on the map, allowing them to head straight to town. *I see! How convenient,* Daisy mused. Genopsyko's insistence had been worth it, then. *All right, let's cross the grasslands and head to the town.*

They started walking, but within five minutes, a hindrance appeared.

"Whoa, they're red!" said Genopsyko.

"Eugh." Nokko grimaced. "Kinda creepy."

They must have hit a spawn area. Hordes of skeletons were crawling up out of the ground. What's more, unlike the pure white ones from the wasteland, these were covered in brilliant red.

"Skeleton mark two, huh?" said @Meow-Meow.

"So they're just doing a palette-swap to cut down on the work, huh?" Genopsyko griped. "That's a pretty cheap technique for a magical game."

"Everyone, stay alert," said Daisy. "We're in a new area, so the enemies may have gotten stronger. Don't judge a book by its cover. Fight with all you have!"

Genopsyko dropped her visor, @Meow-Meow raised her leg and struck a kung fu pose, and Nokko lifted her ribbon-adorned mop. They'd already discussed their strategy for these monsters.

Visor lowered, Genopsyko charged in first. Her magic lay in her special suit. According to her, it could protect her from even a supernova or the Big Bang itself. As long as her visor was down, no attack could get through. Daisy wondered if it would even stop her Daisy Beam, but she never said it out loud. She was the adult here, so she had to act like one and not mess with the other girl.

Genopsyko rushed in, kicking, punching, and pummeling everything within reach. The gun at her hip was just a decoration to help sell the theme, so she left it there and opted for hand-to-hand combat. She investigated thoroughly to see how the enemy would attack and how hard they would hit. "Hey, looks like there's no need to worry! These things aren't much different from the white versions!" she reported.

Next, @Meow-Meow hit a skeleton with a flying kick, while Nokko spun her mop, destroying a crimson skull. Naturally, Daisy wasn't just standing there, either. She hit the monsters with

everything she'd practiced, from elbow strikes to roundhouse kicks, palm strikes, and front kicks. In the blink of an eye, the enemies had scattered, and only one remained.

"Everyone, spread out! I'm gonna finish this!" Making sure everyone was out of the way, Magical Daisy pointed at the skeleton and shouted. She could have just attacked, but her fans were here. It would be a discredit to her name not to end things with her finishing move and a little fan service.

"Daisy Beam!" The yellow ray struck the skeleton right in the torso. She'd imagined its spine vaporizing, ribs flying as red bones clattered to the ground, but the thing continued on undamaged. @Meow-Meow jumped in, delivering kicks to the heel, hips, and neck in quick succession and destroying it entirely.

Genopsyko was pointing at Magical Daisy and shouting something. For some reason, Daisy couldn't hear. Something welled up inside her throat, then forced its way out. Warm liquid. She could see the sky. It was pure blue, not a single cloud there. Something hit her back. As she fell, she caught a glimpse of her stomach. It was stained bright red, blood pouring out of it with no sign of stopping.

Finally, her heart gave one last big pulse, and her consciousness faded.

☆ Pechka

With the town as their base, the party hunted for monsters on the grasslands and built up their candy stash. They also simultaneously explored to gain information on the area quest or other useful hints for completing the game. It was risky to break up the party, but with the map they'd rolled from R, they could keep track of one another's positions, so they ended up splitting into two teams. When it was decided that they'd split into a fighting pair and a scouting pair, Pechka breathed a deep sigh of relief.

She wasn't brave enough to fight or thick-skinned enough to withstand the condemning stares for her lack of contribution. Rionetta had even commented in a stage whisper, likely so Pechka would overhear, "Perhaps it would be more *efficient* if we only had three in our party."

If Pechka had been brave enough, she would have spat back, "*I don't remember asking to join, stupid,*" and then things wouldn't have turned out like this.

There wasn't much she could do, so she didn't really do anything. Time went on by anyway. She wanted to hurry up and finish the game, but it didn't feel like they were making any progress. The only change she really felt was her rising frustration. When it would finally bubble over, even Pechka didn't know.

She volunteered herself for the scouting party.

"Ha-ha-ha! I will get so much useful information, even the doll will be *surprise*!" Nonako Miyokata wasn't all that intimidating compared with Rionetta and her sharp tongue or Clantail and her silent pressure. Nonako looked human, at least, compared with the two monster girls.

"The grasslands are so *agréable*! Let's never go back to that wasteland!"

"Um, could you try to be a little quieter...?" Pechka trailed off.

"I hope there will be living creatures here, *t'sais*? I'm gonna adopt them!"

"Um..."

"Pechka, how did you become a girl *magique*? I received an e-mail."

"Like I said..."

"This is so cute! Cuteness is *la justice*!"

"Hey, please don't pull..."

She was so loud. As they explored, Nonako Miyokata never shut her mouth, oblivious to Pechka and her ever-present anxiety that the extra noise would attract monsters. When the scenery changed, Nonako would instantly start babbling. When the wind blew, she laughed. And even when absolutely nothing was happening, she continued to ramble on about herself. Apparently, she had a very cute friend named Tama, but she had been unable to bring it with her into the game. According to Fal, all they were allowed to bring in was their weapons and costumes.

All this was more exhausting than the walking. Her fatigue made the rations taste much better, but Pechka wasn't happy about that.

"So then they should send more than just skeletons!" They were eating the dry and tasteless rations atop some rocks when—*bam*! Nonako smacked the stone beneath her. Pechka was so startled she dropped her food. She quickly scooped it up and blew on it before resuming her meal.

"With only these skeletons, I can't use my *magique*! If I could make a friend, I could finally be useful to this *ensemble*. No one needs a magical girl who can't use her ability!"

What must she think of Pechka, then, whose ability to create good food was of no real use to the party? She was too scared to ask.

"That's why I am searching for new *monstres* during this investigation," Nonako proclaimed, clenching a fist. Her eyes shone. "Pechka, if you find one, then please let *moi* take it. As thanks, I will defend you if the others try to kick you out."

"Oh…sure. Thanks."

Nonako grabbed her hand and shook it. Pechka guessed that was her attempt to cheer her up. But she was going about it rather oddly, and Pechka didn't feel very encouraged.

This place seemed to have more potential to host living things than the wasteland did. But despite Nonako's enthusiastic babbling about how there had to be animal-type monsters, they never saw anything other than red skeletons—not even an ant.

"*Putain*! This game is *conneries*!" Nonako muttered, and Pechka nodded. No animal-type monsters appeared—fortunately for Pechka, who was scared of them, but unfortunately for Nonako, who wanted some companions. But they were able to meet other players.

Pfle, the magical girl in a wheelchair they'd met in town, said she was in the middle of completing the quest to unlock the next area. The other members of her party were out collecting candy.

Pfle looked so evanescent, like she'd disappear under the lightest touch, and so helpless, like she'd break under a caress. Pechka wondered if it was okay to let her attempt the quest by herself, but Pfle's strong voice belied her appearance. *She's a magical girl, too, after all*, thought Pechka.

"It seems a few parties have already formed, and there's one girl out on her own as well," Pfle had informed them.

Out on her own. Just thinking about being forced to fight the skeletons all by herself sent a chill up Pechka's spine. That was the last thing she wanted.

"One group is hunting to the east of town, and another is doing the same to the south," Pfle added. "Oddly enough, no one's staking claim to territories yet. We're all naturally keeping our distances. Oh, and there are red skeletons in these grasslands. Be careful of them."

"But they are weaklings. No *différent* from the white ones!"

"Unlike the white ones, they have the ability to reflect projectiles," said Pfle. She held out her magical phone to show them an illustration depicting a red skeleton. The impressive image of the skeleton poised to attack looked stronger than the real ones that just broke apart.

Name: Powered Skeleton. Magical candy: 8–12. Spawn area: Grasslands. Group numbers: 5–20. Elemental weakness: Fire. Can reflect any long-range attack. Use close-quarters combat to defeat them.

The entry went on and on.

"One of our party members threw a rock at them," explained Pfle. "She now has a big lump on her head."

"What is this? Data *de les monstres*?"

"A monster encyclopedia. It's an app for sale in the shop. You might need it if we're going to start encountering abilities like Attack Reflection. It wouldn't be pretty if one of your attacks bounced back at you."

Pechka and Nonako immediately messaged Clantail, notifying her of the red skeleton's ability to reflect projectiles. Their party had long ago exchanged numbers. The e-mail app still seemed to be broken, but for some reason it could still send messages to other people inside the game just fine.

"You should check out the grasslands shop. There are a lot of items for sale. Weapons and armor and such, too. The material and make of them are rather plain for magical-girl equipment, though. A bit lacking, I suppose."

Pechka jotted down what Pfle had said in her phone's notepad, and they bid good-bye to the other girl. Their information exchange had been entirely one-sided, since Pfle had already known everything they had to share in return, but Pfle still smiled and waved good-bye at them.

"She was *très* nice!" said Nonako.

"Yes, I'm so glad we ran into such a good person," Pechka agreed.

Pfle was the only magical girl they met on their scouting mission. Perhaps the others were all busy killing monsters on their hunting grounds. The bounty the grasslands offered compared to the wasteland made it easy to assume the others would also want to farm candy for a bit.

Messages filled the town. There were no signs of life, only haphazardly arranged buildings, but posters and little notes doled out hints everywhere. There was a variety of messages—not just ones like *This is the grasslands town*, but also things like *Monsters appear in X area, so be careful* and *Each town's shop sells different items*. Pechka recorded each and every one.

"I do not like this."

"Huh? Why?" asked Pechka.

"There are no dressers or treasure chests in *les maisons*! Fishing through others' things with no consequences is the privilege only for *un héros*!"

"I'm not sure about that..."

Despite Nonako's complaints, Pechka figured they had basically done all right. They picked up a letter in one of the houses and followed the instructions inside, bringing it to a building in the wasteland town. They were awarded with one hundred pieces of magical candy.

"*La mission* was a big success!" Nonako clapped.

It's less that she's loud. More like she's just very emotive, Pechka thought.

Night fell, so they met up with the combat party at their prede-termined meeting spot in front of the grasslands town. There they sat in a circle, exchanging the information they'd gathered and dis-cussing the candy haul. Conventionally, a party would sit around a campfire, but magical girls had excellent night vision, and they didn't need to scare off animals or worry about warmth, so their little ring was empty.

Rionetta seemed very tired. Her expression was less than lively, and she hardly said a word. Clantail's silence was normal for her, but her tiny deer tail was drooping weakly, and she looked exhausted, too.

Pechka had assumed that fighting had sapped their energy, but apparently, that was not the case.

"We were hardly able to earn a thing," said Rionetta.

"Oh?" said Nonako. "Who was going on about those who don't work?"

"It wasn't that we weren't making an effort. We simply couldn't." Every time they found a new hunting ground, some other magical girl was already there and chased them off.

"What nasty people, *oui*."

"Indeed. Almost as nasty as you."

Before Nonako could retort, Clantail stomped her hoof against the ground. Halfway to her feet, Nonako sat back down. Rionetta closed her mouth.

Pechka munched on her meal, quaking in her boots. No mat-ter how hungry she was, the food was so flavorless that she couldn't enjoy it. *Still*, Pechka thought, *Rionetta's stubborn, and Clantail isn't the type to let such a crazy demand slide. If someone told them to go away, would they actually just do it?* Seeing how tired they both were, it was possible something else had happened.

As Pechka chewed and thought, her magical phone rang. And not just hers—the others' devices went off, too. On the screen were instructions:

A game event is now beginning. All players will be
transported to the square of the wasteland town in five minutes.

☆ **Shadow Gale**

Just like when they'd first started the game, the scenery changed instantaneously. The sudden change made Shadow Gale's feet unsteady, so she grabbed on to the back of the wheelchair to keep from falling. This was that forcible transportation, all right.

Magical girls filled the square. It was quite a spectacle to see so many magical girls in one place, even in a game. A shrine maiden–looking girl was facing one who resembled a samurai and shouting a strange string of words like "Geisha! Hara-kiri! Divine redistribution!" But the samurai girl was ignoring her.

Three girls—one dressed like a maid, one in battle-force style, and the other in a Chinese dress—were sitting in a corner, apparently discussing something. Maybe it was just Shadow Gale's imagination, but they all seemed ragged and pale. Chatting with them was a girl with a deerstalker cap and cape...rather resembling a certain famous detective.

A girl with the lower half of a deer was flicking her tail back and forth. Perhaps she was excited. On the other hand, her companion, a cook or pastry chef of some sort, appeared uneasy.

Shadow Gale observed them all, somewhat fascinated. One girl caught her eye. She gave Pfle's sleeve a couple of tugs and whispered, "That's it. That's her."

The girl she was eyeing was encased in a fluffy, fuzzy plush hamster suit and munching on a giant sunflower seed. Another girl with a huge bow slung over her back was standing next to her and talking at her, but it was hard to tell if the hamster girl was listening.

"Yes, there's no doubt. Different size, though." Masked Wonder seconded Shadow Gale's statement.

While Pfle was busy gathering information, Shadow Gale and Masked Wonder had been grinding for candy—in other words, hunting down monsters and fighting them nonstop. Even in a game, the constructs of capitalist and laborer, white collar and blue collar, user and used, remained.

They ran around the endless field of grass from end to end, exploring all corners of the area until they encountered the steep cliffs acting as boundaries, defeating every red skeleton they met along the way. They were taking a break to eat when it happened.

Masked Wonder noticed it first. "...What *is* that?"

Shadow Gale followed her gaze. Masked Wonder placed her palm on the ground, watching it closely. Shadow Gale did the same. It wasn't obvious at first, but eventually, she could feel the slowly swelling tremors. A tremendous, rhythmic thumping shook the ground, growing gradually larger and larger.

"Look over there," Masked Wonder prompted, and Shadow Gale followed the other girl's gaze. Something was advancing from the horizon toward them. It looked like a monster—but also like a magical girl.

Shadow Gale rubbed her eyes and did a double take. "Uh...is something weird going on with perspective, here?"

"It seems right to me."

It was big—leagues wider and taller than Masked Wonder, Pfle, and Shadow Gale. They could feel the tremors getting stronger, shaking the ground hard enough to lift Shadow Gale's bottom clear off the ground. How many creatures on the planet were capable of creating minor earthquakes just by running?

It came to a point about a hundred yards away from them and then stopped. But even that far away, they had to crane their necks to see the top. The creature—no, the *monolith*—had to be over thirty yards tall. "You're not allowed to hunt here!" it yelled. Its voice was big, too. The grass around them trembled with every word. Shadow Gale felt like she was about to be blown away herself and instinctively lowered her center of gravity.

"Cherna's group found this place first, so it's our territory. So stay out!" the giant yelled. It was insisting they leave the hunting grounds. In other words, it wasn't a monster, but a magical girl.

"There's nothing in this game's rules that says you can blame us for that!" Masked Wonder shouted. She wasn't about to bow to this giant.

And she didn't have to bow, but Shadow Gale wished she would just back off. Shadow Gale's legs were shaking, and tears were welling in her eyes. While she agreed that this nonsense about territories was unfair and Masked Wonder was simply saying out loud what Shadow Gale was thinking, she also knew full well that being in the right did not mean you would win. What was she doing picking a fight with a ninety-foot colossus?

"If you don't leave, you'll make Cherna angry!" As a demonstration of that fury, she stomped her foot, and the ground shook.

Shadow Gale toppled onto the grass. "We can't. We can't take her." She shuffled along on her knees to cling to Masked Wonder's cape, tugging on it. "That's not something we can fight. Let's run away. Nobody's going to pat your back for fighting, and there's no point. Please, let's just run."

Masked Wonder brushed her hand off and adopted a battle stance. "Might does not make right. But justice without strength is meaningless."

"I'm telling you, it's hopeless!"

"I am the Masked Wonder! A magical girl, the embodiment of justice and strength!" she shouted, jumping up. And up. And up and up... Shadow Gale's eyes went wide with surprise. She still hadn't come back down. The launch itself had seemed light enough, but the distance and speed defied the laws of physics as she hurtled the one hundred yards to her target, landing a kick on the giant magical girl's chest. Frozen in the face of that sudden, massive leap, the giant just stood there and took the kick—though it looked less like a kick and more like a light touch. But it sent the giantess flying like a feather until she landed on her knees thirty yards back.

Such an enormous object hitting the ground after a ninety-yard flight should have caused a quake far greater than her steps had, but the giant hardly made a sound as she floated down. She seemed confused, too. She cocked her head to the side, patting herself down. "What did you do? Is this your magic?"

"We will not bend to your threats!"

Shadow Gale didn't mind being part of this "we," but more

than that, she was impressed with how amazingly Masked Wonder had fought. She dazedly stared at the battle between the titan and the superheroine.

"So threats aren't enough, huh?" The giant stood up and swiftly spun her right arm to create a gust. Shadow Gale threw herself down on the ground and clung to the grass, but it felt like the roots were about to give way.

"Just try it. If you think you can beat me, that is." Masked Wonder readied herself.

The tension in the air was thick, the situation inches from an explosion, when someone yelled, "Wait!"

That wasn't Masked Wonder's voice, and neither was it the goliath's bellow. Shadow Gale was too rattled to have said anything. That was when she first noticed. Someone was standing on the giantess's shoulder—and they dropped something from above.

Thinking it was an attack, Shadow Gale backed away and watched the object fall. It was a blue gem about the size of a baby's fist. Not a raw gem, either, but carefully cut so that every angle shined. If it was real, how much was it worth? It had to be a fake.

"Hup!" A girl wearing a blue dress and a cape of white fur, with a black-and-white-striped tail growing from her behind—clearly a magical girl—was standing where there had been nothing before. Shadow Gale retreated even farther.

Pinkie and index finger extended on each hand, the newcomer crossed her arms in front of her face, bent her right knee, and stretched out her left leg. The pose looked strenuous. "The blue flash descends on the battlefield! Lapis Lazuline!"

Masked Wonder strode toward her, raised her right arm, bent her left in front of her chest, braced her legs in a wide stance, and struck her "victory pose." "I am the Masked Wonder! A magical girl, the embodiment of powerful justice!"

They stared at each other for a few seconds. Then they relaxed at the same time, extended their right hands, and shook. Shadow Gale didn't really get it, but the two seemed to have come to an understanding.

The girl who had introduced herself as Lapis Lazuline scooped up the gem and turned back to the giant. "Hey! Ya can head back, Cherny! No need to fight these people!" Her tone was quite flippant, despite her dramatic entrance.

"But, but Melville said to guard the hunting ground!" the enormous girl protested.

"Nay." That was another voice.

Looking toward the sound, Shadow Gale could see a faded figure melting into the grasslands. Little by little, the image patched together, and the green faded, revealing a magical girl. In her right hand was a longbow that looked out of place in her thin arms, and in her left hand she clasped an equally out of place rustic harpoon. Contrasting with her heavy weapons were a light gray cape, supple legs extending from her short skirt, vines with blooming purple roses winding through her reddish-brown hair, and pointed elf ears. All of these made it clear she was a magical girl.

Is making dramatic entrances a requirement to be part of this magical-girl party? Shadow Gale wondered.

"Th' strong rule in th' mountains, lest ye be eten. None but th' most stout o' hairt are free to hunt 'ere in this land. If ye nae be strong, ye cannae be permi'ed."

Shadow Gale frowned. Looking at this girl filled her with unease. Was it just her strong accent? Or was it her oddly calm voice? The fact that she'd appeared out of nowhere? Shadow Gale glanced to Masked Wonder—she was perfectly calm. Unperturbed, she crossed her arms. This had the side effect of emphasizing her large breasts.

"Melvy's sayin' ya can use this place, since you're strong," Lapis Lazuline translated.

In response, the girl Lapis Lazuline had called Melvy nodded with a grunt. "Godspeed." The girl's body turned green again, faded into the grass, and eventually vanished.

Lapis Lazuline scaled her way up the giantess, grabbing hold of her shoulder again. "Well, see ya 'round. Bye!"

The giantess sprinted off, her footsteps shaking the ground, just like when she'd come. From her shoulder, Lapis Lazuline waved. The pair grew smaller and smaller, until eventually they disappeared beyond the horizon. Shadow Gale looked at Masked Wonder and saw that she was waving back.

Shadow Gale finished recounting the events of the previous day, and Pfle gave a light nod in response. Though it had already been three days since the game had started, Pfle's levelheaded attitude showed no signs of flagging.

"She's small now, which means she must use magic to grow," said Pfle. "That would be difficult to use in the real world due to how much attention it would attract. But in a game world, she can blow herself up as big as she wants without worrying that people will see."

"It was quite shocking! No match for me, though," said Masked Wonder.

"And the disappearing girl," Pfle went on. "That sounds like optical camouflage rather than invisibility. Being able to change her color would fit that."

"That seems pretty useful! Of course, no match for me, though."

"Exactly. You're as strong as I knew you would be. That's the strength you need as an enforcer of justice. I'm not just talking about muscular or magical strength, either. You have a strong heart."

Masked Wonder's cheeks flushed red, and the tip of her nose seemed to rise by half an inch. Pfle knew exactly how to butter her up.

And that was right when a magical girl walked over to them. Pinkie and index finger extended on both hands, she crossed them in front of her face, bent her right knee, and extended her left leg. "The blue flash descends on the battlefield! Lapis Lazuline!"

Matching her, Masked Wonder raised her right arm, crooked her left arm in front of her chest, and spread her legs wide in her "victory pose." "I am the Masked Wonder! A magical girl, the embodiment of powerful justice!"

They stared at each other for a few seconds before relaxing at the same time, smiling as they shook hands. Were they planning

to do this every single time they ran into each other? Shadow Gale wished they would at least show a little restraint when they were in front of so many people.

"Well, well, well! Thank you all so very much for coming, pon." A voice came from her magical phone. Shadow Gale only knew one person—creature...thing?—that said "pon," and in that cheerful tone.

Shadow Gale took out her phone and pointed it upward to see a hologram rise from the screen. The black-and-white sphere floated lightly in the air. Similar images stood above the others' phones. They were all saying the same thing.

"Today is logout day, pon. You will all be logged out at exactly sunset. We plan to spend three days of real-world time doing maintenance before you may log in again, pon. Going forward, we will be keeping to this same schedule as you play the game, pon." Fal twirled around, scattering gold scales into the air. "Usually, there will be a special event on logout days. These range from very lucky to very unlucky events. One will be chosen at random, pon. Today...*ho-ho*! My, my, my. A very lucky draw indeed, pon. There's a very kind message in the grasslands settlement with the name of the town on it. Have you all seen it, pon? I want you to all go to where that message is right now, pon. The first one to reach it will receive a special, rare item from Fal—"

Not waiting for Fal to finish, Pfle shot off like a rocket, leaving dust clouds in her wake. A second later, the rest of the girls followed after her like a stampede. Shadow Gale and the remaining few watched them go.

No one could beat Pfle's speed, and she'd even gotten a head start on them, so the event ended with a crushing victory for her. She'd taken a lead of more than a thousand lengths.

After the event was over, Shadow Gale was relieved that no one seemed angry about Pfle jumping the gun. The next time a similar event came up, however, many were sure to cheat in the same way, which disheartened her. People like Pfle seemed to always be setting bad precedents.

The rare item she received for winning was a coin. On the front was a girl holding up an obviously magical stick—a staff. The back was engraved with a star. Gleaming golden, it was about the same size as a five-hundred-yen coin, albeit much heavier. Suspecting it might be pure gold, Shadow Gale inspected it, but she had no skill for appraisal. She didn't feel like biting it like someone out of a period piece, either. That probably wouldn't tell her anything, anyway.

"That's the Miracle Coin, pon," Fal informed them. "If you carry that, enemy drop rates will increase slightly, pon."

"Drop rates?" asked Pfle. "You mean we'll get more candy?"

"No, no. Certain enemies can drop items other than candy, pon. Some enemies even drop *super*-rare items on *super*-rare occasions, pon. That coin will surely come in handy when trying to collect those, pon. To give you a hard number, it will bump up the drop rate by about five times, pon."

Pfle transferred her prize from her phone to Masked Wonder's. Now the Miracle Coin was inside her phone's item bank. Just like the map, potions, and passes, it had to go inside a phone before it could be used. Apparently, that was the standard in this game. She could withdraw it by selecting it from the inventory.

"I'll have Masked Wonder use the coin. I take it you're fine with that?" said Pfle.

Not that she'd care if I said I wasn't, Shadow Gale thought. But honestly, she had no complaints. More often than not, Masked Wonder was the one with the chance to land the finishing blow on enemies.

"I won't waste this rare item you've granted me. You can count on me!" As Masked Wonder struck her victory pose, her breasts jiggled.

MASTER SIDE #2

"What's the meaning of this, pon? Did Fal perhaps mishear something?"

Countless monitors filled the room in systematic lines, displaying countless areas from within *Magical Girl Raising Project*, such as the wasteland, the grasslands, the interior of the towns, and other yet-undiscovered areas, as if it were all being recorded through security cameras. Monitors were embedded into each wall and buried in the floor and ceiling, covering every surface to light the room.

"You didn't mishear aaanything," the girl said, in the middle of solving a Rubik's Cube. Forgoing the normal method of solving it with one's hands, she had precariously balanced a corner of the cube on her index finger. As she stared at it, the cube moved at a steady pace, piecing patterns together by itself.

On the desk was a pair of glasses, next to which was a magical phone propped up against a monitor. Above it, a hologram of Fal floated at an angle. The dust drifting in the air, illuminated by the hologram, spoke volumes about the hygienic state of the area.

The hologram shuddered wildly. It twisted, bent, and returned to its original form, though not without some static. "This isn't what we talked about, pon. No one was supposed to die, pon.

You said there'd be no feedback from damage going to their real bodies."

"Nothing about the concept has changed."

"If people knew it was that kind of game, they would never participate, pon."

"But they don't *have* a choice, duh. They can't do aaanything to stop it. I'm not gonna let them."

"The Magical Kingdom won't just sit quietly and let this happen, pon!" Fal howled. The timbre of its synthetic voice deepened to sound more like an adult male's.

Unperturbed, the girl's eyes remained fixed on the Rubik's Cube. "I'm not gonna report it, siiilly. And you're not allowed to tell the players, either. You're just a mascot. You don't have the capabilities to disobey your master, so you *can't* report it. Nope, nooope!"

"What are you thinking, pon? Is this some sick joke, pon? Save your humor for someone else, pon."

"I'm nooot joking around. The real joke here is the Magical Kingdom, ignoring their children."

"Fal understands your concerns, master. The children may be dangerous, pon. Yet the Magical Kingdom has covered their ears and won't listen. So we have to make sure ourselves. Fal understands, pon. Fal gets it, pon. That's exactly why this is—"

"The children just have to prove to us that they're real magical girls."

The only sound that followed her remarks was the clicking of the Rubik's Cube.

CHAPTER 3
THE DETECTIVE AND THE MURDER CASE

☆ Detec Bell

Detec Bell was a detective.

Equipped with her deerstalker cap, prop pipe, and magnifying glass, she looked just like a female Holmes. But she wasn't merely a magical girl with a detective-themed costume. She was a detective, because Shinobu Hioka, when she wasn't transformed into Detec Bell, actually worked as one.

Shinobu had a brother who was four years her elder. When she had been in kindergarten, she'd followed him everywhere, much to his displeasure, but follow him eagerly she did. She even tagged along during his bus trip with the local children's club. The club was supposed to be for elementary school kids, but she'd thrown a fit, screaming and crying and wailing that it was unfair and mean that only her brother got to go. Her force of will overwhelmed her

father, who ended up negotiating with the head of the neighborhood association on her behalf.

The excursion was to a farm in a neighboring town. It was
spring, and the bright sun was warm and perfect for children to
frolic in. They bubbled at the sight of cows, shouted when watching
the horses, fed the sheep and rabbits, got to try milking cows, and
then clambered onto the bus to head back home. That was when
Shinobu encountered her destiny.

Shinobu was watching a rerun of some anime on the on-board
TV while the other kids slept, exhausted. The night before, she had
been so excited for the excursion, she'd gone straight to sleep after
dinner and then slept like a log right up until they left for the trip,
so she still had plenty of energy left even after all the excitement of
the farm.

On-screen, a child detective was solving a locked-room mystery. To Shinobu at the time, they might as well have been recit-
ing a list of technical vocabulary. She didn't understand what the
characters were saying, but she saw a child her age dismantling
the plots of adults and getting praise, even respect, from them and
the older detectives around him. As for his weapons, he had a few
secret tools, reliable allies, and above all, his brilliant mind.

To a kindergarten-aged child, the term "murderer" was more
exciting than "world domination" or "the extinction of humanity."
The kid on-screen was a hero for fighting criminals like murderers.
Swept up in the emotions of the story, Shinobu's hands balled into
fists amid the snores inside the bus.

Shinobu became a huge fan of that boy detective and got her
brother to borrow the original manga from his friends. She read
every volume. Luckily, it came with pronunciation guides, so even
when she couldn't read the words, at least she could sound it out.
"Alibi," "plot twist," "locked-room mystery"—the many fascinat-
ing phrases captured her imagination. She stopped following her
brother around. He claimed it was a relief, but he also looked a bit
disappointed...or maybe that was just what Shinobu wanted to
believe.

She asked her father to rent the DVDs, and once she'd seen every single episode and movie, her interests moved to the mystery genre in general. That was when she started on her father's personal collection. His bookshelf, created from cheap colored shelves on a Sunday afternoon, was filled with mystery series. But when he found her reading his books, he confiscated them with an admonishment that they were for adults. So she turned to reading them in secret. There were no pronunciation guides in these, so she had to learn as she went. The words she couldn't understand she assumed from context, and while the other children were glued to anime and shows with flashy special effects, she was hiding alone and reading her mystery novels.

Her favorites were the ones with kid detectives. In the anime she'd first fallen in love with, the detective was never wrong—a perfect jack-of-all-trades. Throughout elementary and middle school, she read detective novels day and night, and in high school she founded a mystery fan club. One investigator solved locked-room mysteries with a superior brain and intellect, always finding the killer. In another, the hero struggled against a powerful organization for no reward in order to save a helpless girl. The adventures of these tough, cool detectives made her heart race.

For the high school culture festival, her club put on a dramatic adaptation of the famous detective novel *Village of Eight Gravestones* and covered the gym in gore. The PE teacher chewed them out for that one, but the over-the-top production was a success, and the audience really had a good time. Oh, the enthusiastic storm of applause for Shinobu as she played Kosuke Kindaichi! Just remembering it gave her a shot of euphoria.

This was what it was like to be a detective. No—being a real gumshoe had to be even more amazing. Maybe this should have steered Shinobu toward the path of an actress, but it only strengthened her resolve to work as an investigator herself.

Ignoring her parents' objections, Shinobu got a job at a detective agency straight out of junior college. That was three years ago. Soon after, she happened to receive a message inviting her to take part in the magical-girl selection test. She made it through the trials and finally got her powers. Shinobu was sure that her newfound status would help her solve mysteries. First and foremost, she was a detective.

She still remembered vividly the first time she had transformed into a magical girl.

She was beautiful. Shinobu wasn't really the type to long for looks or beauty, but it still left a big impression on her. Just looking in the mirror was enough to set her heart racing. She stretched a little in an attempt to distract herself and found that her every movement left a fruity, sweet, and pleasant fragrance in the air.

The message hadn't been a joke or prank. She pinched her cheek to see if she was dreaming or hallucinating, but the pain said otherwise. This was clearly impossible, scientifically speaking. But Shinobu had become a real, true, authentic, genuine magical girl.

Detec Bell's costume was more subdued than those of the other magical girls, which allowed her to blend in with the regular people in town and do her job. Her physical abilities, however, far surpassed any other living creature's, and her enhanced endurance allowed her to work for days without rest. Her night vision was excellent, too—she could see as well at night as she could during the day. These were all great skills for tracking clues.

Every magical girl possessed a unique ability, and Shinobu's was perfect for her detective work. With her magic, she could solve any locked-room mystery and any seemingly impossible crime. No criminal could escape her.

Unfortunately, none of her detective work involved locked-room mysteries or grand capers. She'd worked at the agency for three years. She was perfect at tailing and stakeouts, thanks to her magic. Her clients loved her, and some even offered to fund her to go independent. But she was also learning the reality of being a detective.

Shinobu would have been fine with just investigating cheating spouses and searching for runaways, but new recruits like her were stuck on filing and phone duty. Her superiors constantly demanded she clean and serve tea. And on top of more miscellaneous tasks, she was also forced to watch pets, assist in house cleaning, and even carry boxes for people when they moved. Her superiors worked her to the bone. Her boss was a kind-looking old man who would tell her things like "This'll be good for you" and "This is the first step to becoming a first-class detective" while ordering her to do petty tasks. The juxtaposition of his looks and his unconvincing remarks made him a particularly nasty boss to have.

But Shinobu still knew who she was. She knew the true experience of being a detective, but she hadn't abandoned her dream. She would always aspire to solve mysteries, and she liked herself for taking the steps to make it reality.

Magical Daisy ended up failing out of the game.

She had tried to show off by shooting a monster with her Daisy Beam, but it ended up ricocheting right back at her due to the ability of the "powered skeleton" to reflect projectile attacks. One shot had finished her.

After interviewing her party members, investigating the scene, and analyzing the body, Shinobu had determined this story to be true. All the evidence pointed to an accidental death, and there was no possibility of it being premeditated murder.

But the fact that it was unintentional wasn't the issue. The real problem lay elsewhere.

Immediately after logging out of the game, Shinobu requested some time off. Her boss yelled at her over the phone. "You think we can afford to give you three days off when we're so busy?"

Shinobu gave him some flimsy *"Yes, sir, of course, sir"* lines and then turned off her flip phone's power. Unfortunately for him, her day job was not her highest priority.

First, she searched the Internet for "Magical Kingdom" and how to contact them on her special phone. She had a ton of questions for them, but for some reason, all her messages bounced back. After a lot of trying and failing, she gave up on that angle and focused on scouring the web.

She typed "Magical Daisy," added a space and a few search keywords, and pressed ENTER. One site caught her attention with an article discussing how the background in the *Magical Daisy* anime resembled a certain train station. This complemented the information Shinobu had gotten from Genopsyko Yumenoshima.

After compiling her search results, she learned which location the show's setting was based on. Apparently, among the more hard-core fans, it was celebrated as a holy land. Even years after its original airing, *Magical Daisy* was still relatively popular in the early-morning Sunday kids' anime slot, but these days, no one was raving about the holy land anymore.

Closing her magical phone, Shinobu transformed. She pulled her cap low over her head so as to appear inconspicuous, threw her wallet and other necessities into her work bag, and left her apartment complex.

She rode the bullet train headed for Tohoku, transferred to a regular train, then switched again to private rail and rode three stops down to an empty station. After dropping her ticket into the turnstile, she stepped out into B City, B Prefecture. Checking her surroundings to be sure no one was looking, she lightly kissed the station wall. A caricature of a human visage appeared on the cracked and dirty surface. It resembled a shabby middle-aged man, more like something from anime or manga than real life. The face her magic summoned differed from object to object.

Huh, so this is the one you get from an old, empty station like this, she thought.

The eyes of the three-foot-wide cartoon goggled as they landed on Detec Bell. "What do you want?" It was mumbling. Every object was different in this regard.

"Have you heard of Magical Daisy?"

"No."

"It's this girl." Using her phone, Detec Bell showed the face a picture of Magical Daisy.

"Oh, I know her. She's helped out some people in this station."

"Okay, thanks." She gave the face another kiss, this time on the tip of its nose, and it melted back into the wall. This was Detec Bell's magical ability: conversing with buildings. There were some conditions. For one, it required a kiss to both activate and stop, and for another, objects would never incriminate their owners, but still, it was quite valuable in her detective work.

Incidentally, when she had tried using her magic on the dilapidated buildings within the game, they had replied coldly to her, "I am master's property. I cannot speak on topics against master's will. Please search for hints on completing the game through regular means." She'd used her magic on the other buildings, too, but while they all spoke in different tones, they offered basically the same explanation. She was disappointed she couldn't use her magic to get some easy hints.

After leaving the station, Shinobu stopped by a nearby convenience store and bought a local newspaper. In the sticks, these kinds of shops sat on huge plots of land with similarly large parking lots. Leaning against a cement barrier, she opened the newspaper.

Shinobu had learned from Nokko that Daisy had been in middle school while the *Magical Daisy* anime was on air. This meant Shinobu could reverse-calculate her age. Being in middle school, there was no way she could have done her magical girl work far away from home. She had to have been active in her local neighborhood. As long as they hadn't moved, her family would still be here.

Magical girls also needed a place to transform without being seen. They were cautious about human witnesses, but nobody ever thought about the buildings. There had to be one in the area that had witnessed Magical Daisy transform. Asking structure after structure, Shinobu traced the path Daisy had gone as her magical-girl self. Eventually, she would reach her home. If the person in question wasn't there, Shinobu would pursue the possibility that the family had moved. If they had, a building had to have seen it—and the brick and concrete never forgot.

The purpose of this investigation was to ascertain whether Magical Daisy was alive or dead in this world. Personally, Shinobu hoped she was alive. Fal had insisted that feedback from in-game damage wouldn't affect their real bodies. That was the whole reason she'd agreed to participate in the game in the first place. This was ultimately just to assuage her doubts, just to make sure that no mistakes had cropped up anywhere. All that pushed her along was an uneasy feeling. She had no basis for her doubts, and she was fully aware of that.

Detec Bell folded up the newspaper and threw it into her bag. She had three days.

☆ **Pechka**

Just like before, Pechka changed clothes and went to give Ninomiya her homemade lunch. When she cut in line, no one complained. She could only hear them whispering "It's that girl again" and "Who is she?" The first time, it had made her proud and happy and excited, though with a pain deep in her heart, and later, she'd floundered on her bed. Now, the second time, she didn't feel any of those things.

The autumn sun set early. Darkness was quickly setting in, and the public playground was empty of children. The only one there was Pechka, sitting on the swings.

Just thinking about the game dampened her mood. Just as Fal had explained, upon hearing the logout announcement, she was instantly on her bed again. A look at the clock showed that the minute hand hadn't even made one full rotation. But that didn't make all of this okay.

She should have declined, but she hadn't been able to. Apparently, one girl had already dropped out of the running. She recalled how depressed that girl's party members had looked. They had been told that in-game damage wouldn't affect them in the real world, but Pechka still didn't like it. The game involved some exploration, of course, but ultimately, it was mainly about fighting, and Pechka wasn't cut out for that.

She sighed.

Maybe it's not too late to back out, she thought, but she was afraid of that, too. The other girls would surely be disappointed in her for dropping out without having contributed. They might badmouth her—maybe even hit or kick her. She knew the damage wouldn't affect her in real life, but pain was still pain. Pinching her cheek hurt just as much in a game as in the real world. Dying in the game had to hurt like real death. Just imagining it upset her. Did the other magical girls just have no imagination?

The concept of a game based around killing enemies or whatever didn't seem fitting for heroines like them. Their job was to help people. Maybe helping people required violence sometimes. But those acts relied on the enhanced strength and magical abilities that they had been granted in order to help people. Maybe it was okay that there were some fringe cases of fighting for the sake of others, but killing enemies to collect candy was not something a magical girl had any business doing.

But even if Pechka were to shout this at the top of her lungs, they would just take it as a weakling's attempts to escape from reality. Nobody would listen to what she had to say. She breathed another sigh.

Maybe she should just focus on the reward. Completing the game would earn her ten million yen. That was so much money, like winning dozens of jumbo lotteries. Her party had agreed that if one of them landed the final blow on the Evil King, they would split the rewards equally among the whole party. In other words, someone like Pechka who didn't want to fight had a chance, but... still, the number didn't seem real to her.

If pushed to say, Pechka might be more glad about the hundred-thousand-yen participation award. Before going out, she'd checked her bank account, and sure enough, the money was there. She could already think of ways to use it. Food she could produce and prepare herself, so that left clothes and accessories such as rings, necklaces, earrings...no, she was a little scared to get pierced, so maybe just clip-ons. Shoes. Bags. Expensive, famous brands that celebrities wore, and the kinds of outfits you saw on models in fashion shows. If the hundred thousand yen wasn't enough, she could always add in some from her new year's gift and her personal savings. Fancy clothes might not look good on Chika, but on Pechka, they did.

Pechka was so consumed by her near-escapist fantasies, she didn't even notice when the sun set.

The shadow she cast under the lamppost's light was stretched

long and came to a point. Hearing the tapping of approaching footsteps, she looked up to see a pair of baseball spikes at the edge of her
shadow. In those shoes was someone wearing a baseball uniform.

Raising her head, Pechka nearly stopped breathing. It was
Ninomiya. His black baseball club bag was hanging off his shoulder. His toned torso, clearly defined even under the uniform,
heaved up and down. He must have been running. There was sweat
on his forehead, and he was looking at Pechka. "Um...," he said,
drawing closer.

Pechka gripped the swing chain tighter. It was covered in thick
plastic, but she could still feel the coldness of the metal beneath.
She realized her temperature was rising.

"You're the girl who brought me lunch, right?" he asked.

She shot up like a spring and nodded repeatedly. All the muscles on her face were as strained as they could be. Her free hand felt
awkwardly empty, so she clenched the skirt of her dress.

"Um, this might sound a bit shameless, but..." He was right in
front of her. He was close enough to touch, close enough that she
could even feel his breath, and she could smell the sweat he'd built
up by running to catch up to her. Ninomiya, the star she'd been
convinced she'd never reach, the boy she'd admired for so long.
She'd never been able to speak to him at school; she'd always just
watched him from afar. Now he was right in front of her.

She was sweating. Her body was on fire. Her heart was racing.
She felt dizzy. Who was it who had said love felt just like the flu?

Ninomiya put a hand behind his head, looking apologetic as he
hesitantly asked, "Would you mind making lunch for me again?"

Pechka nodded over and over. Her tied-up hair bounced up
and down.

"It was *really* good, man. Seriously, like, amazing. Like, I'd
do anything you asked if I could eat that every day. It was crazy
good." The food Pechka's magic created was magically delicious.
Ninomiya did his best to explain just how excellent it had been,
this time adding gestures. "I really wanted to tell you this, but
no one on the team knew who you were. I had to run all over the

neighborhood to find you. Also…could I ask you a favor?" He put his hands together and bowed his head.

Suddenly, Pechka found herself looking down at the back of his head. As was typical for baseball club members, he was forced to keep his hair buzzed short. His head was well shaped, and instead of the usual amusement a buzz cut might elicit, her first thoughts were of how clean it was. It had to be pleasantly fuzzy to the touch. Pechka's right hand moved.

"My teammates liked your food so much that they kept 'sampling' it. I didn't even get to eat the whole thing," he said. Head still low, he chanced a glance up at her. Their eyes met.

Panicking, Pechka pulled her right hand back, but her pulse was rising, her breathing rough as her body attempted to keep up with the demand for oxygen. Ninomiya was looking at her. She'd watched *him* before, but now he was looking at her as she looked at him, and they were staring into each other's eyes.

"In fact," he continued, "there was only scraps by the time I got to it. But still, it was to die for! So I know you might think I'm greedy for asking this, but is there any chance you could give me another? Sometime when no one's looking? I mean, I tried to stop the guys, but they wouldn't listen and basically took everything. I'm serious."

Pechka was so dizzy she was about to faint, but she managed a nod. "Okay." She was so nervous, it came out a bit monotone.

"Really? Seriously? Yes! Thank you so much!" Ninomiya grabbed her hand and shook it, thanking her over and over. Blankly, Pechka stared at him. She was just as dazed when she agreed to meet him in the park again to deliver the lunch. She watched as he scampered off, humming to himself.

Unable to stand anymore, she collapsed back onto the swing set. Her bottom was wet and cold, and she realized how much she'd been sweating. Slowly, the rhythm of her heart calmed, and her burning excitement cooled. She gradually settled down, but even so, the embers still burned deep inside.

Her magic, which she'd only ever considered a bonus, had

turned out to be useful. She'd made Ninomiya happy, and he'd complimented her cooking. He'd even said he would do anything she asked if he could eat it every day.

That was it. Cooking. A path had opened up before her.

☆ Shadow Gale

Until a few years ago, Kanoe's grandfather was the one in charge of the Hitokouji estate. Chronic disease had taken his legs and his sight, and he had needed a special wheelchair to get around, but his mind was healthy as could be. When it came to finance, human resources, investments, contracts, conferences, and a range of other things, his instructions were detailed and precise. There were even rumors that he'd conceived an illegitimate child in his eighties. Considering that the gossip had reached Mamori, it might actually have been true. He had continued to be the brains of the operation until his stroke, and even after his passing, some attributed the stability of the Hitokouji family to his hard work.

Even Kanoe, who was arrogant beyond belief, had been attached to her grandfather. One could see this in the way her manner of speech mirrored his more and more each year. Her parents, her brother, and the other adults in her life let her do it because they found it funny, but for a high school girl, she really talked too much like an old man.

Once Kanoe became a magical girl, her grandfather's presence was clear in her magical-girl costume. The obvious influence was the wheelchair, but its lavish gold construction and fine detail also brought to mind an elderly king on his throne, reigning from the summit of his clan. Her eye patch seemed to represent his diseased eye, and the little birds carved in wood on the wheelchair's fenders looked just like the decorations on the trusty walking stick her grandfather had relied on before losing the use of his legs.

Kanoe's way of life also echoed her grandfather's, Mamori thought. Never hesitating, never deliberating. Or, no—she did mull over things, but she never let anyone see it. She always appeared to instantly know the right answer, which only made people sing her praises ever louder.

But now, Kanoe was dazedly staring out the window of the cooking prep room. It was lunch break, so she was alone. She was clearly lost in thought. Normally, she'd be up to something, like chatting with her classmates in the classroom or speed-reading through books in the library, all the while thinking about something else at a million miles an hour. She never openly worried about anything.

After what had happened the day before, this behavior meant she had to be thinking about the game. And if Kanoe was so invested that she was worrying about it, then that meant Mamori was sure to get dragged in even deeper this time. Mamori was bound to lose weight just thinking about it.

"Trouble builds character. But I think you'll like what I have to say," said Kanoe.

"...Are you a mind reader?" Mamori asked.

"How long do you think I've known you? I can tell that much."

It felt like she was accusing her of being shallow. Mamori was not amused.

Outside the window, some students in their gym clothes were happily chasing a soccer ball. This was a school for rich girls, and there were many different types. It was autumn, but still warm enough that Mamori was impressed they were running around. Watching them made her feel hot, too, so she loosened her scarf.

"It's about the game," said Kanoe.

So Mamori had been right.

"I know you don't like such things," Kanoe continued. "Fighting enemies, grinding for currency, and buying items. With your magic, you don't need to do anything so tedious. You could just use your little cheat to win, but if that's always in the back of your mind, then you'll never enjoy yourself."

"If you want to play the game, miss, then I can't just leave you."

"It's your fault I got dragged into this," she seemed to say with every bit of sarcasm in her body, but Kanoe didn't seem to care about that. Her eyes still on the students running around outside,

she pulled a foot up onto the chair. Her skirt slid to the side, exposing her thighs.

"That's improper, miss," said Mamori.

"There are two types of magical girls."

"Those who fight and those who don't, was it?"

"That game is for those who fight. But that doesn't mean all the participants have to be fighters. There were girls besides you and me who don't fight. So why are they participating?"

"Maybe the reward lured them in."

"Speaking of rewards, we opened up a new area when we were in the game. The prize for that was deposited into one of the accounts I use for foreign trading. I don't know how they found my information, but it was just dropped in there anonymously. Two areas makes two million yen."

"Two million yen! Seriously?"

"It was deposited along with the participation fee. You should check your bank account. And learn to appreciate things other than material rewards."

About five times a month, Mamori found herself wondering how good it would feel to punch Kanoe.

"According to Fal," said Kanoe, "none of the magical girls chosen as test players declined the invite."

"None of them?" That was surprising. It would be natural for at least one or two to reject it after the way they'd been forced into the game. Anyone who would become a magical girl had to have a stubborn will.

"Strange, isn't it? So many players made to participate in such a forceful manner, yet not a single one of them declined. Some of them have to be self-interested types or those who would rather care for flowers than fight. So why didn't anyone decline?"

"You didn't, miss."

"I'm just at that age. I'm aware that I'm unusual."

"Yes, that's for certain."

"It was all just like reality: the smells, the sensations, the sights, the tastes, the sounds. In other words, punches hurt, too.

No matter how convincingly they explained that there would be no damage to your real body, surely that would be reason enough for the nonfighters to balk. So why did they agree to participate?" Kanoe raised her knee higher, and her skirt slid some more. Such careless habits had made her some strange fans here, even though it was a girls' school. "It's ominous."

"I see," Mamori spat out indifferently and turned away. She ended up face-to-face with a skull, but unlike the skeletons in the game, this anatomic model would not be attacking. *I bet she enjoys herself more when things get "ominous,"* she added to herself.

"My magical phone is acting oddly," said Kanoe. "I can't contact the Magical Kingdom."

"Well, my magic can't fix the phones." The devices were magically guarded to protect the information within. When Kanoe had ordered Shadow Gale to use her magic on one before, she'd ended up breaking it entirely. Shadow Gale had managed to lie about the reason for its destruction and receive a replacement—by herself, of course, even though it was originally Kanoe's fault. Just remembering that ticked her off.

"Something doesn't feel right." Kanoe's foot fell from the chair and slapped against the floor, returning her skirt to its original position. Mamori breathed a sigh of relief.

Outside on the field, it seemed things were getting intense. Someone had kicked the ball into the corner of the goal, and all her teammates were high-fiving her. One of the girls noticed them, and her mouth opened in an *ah!* Kanoe smiled back thinly and waved. The students' screech of delight was audible all the way up in the classroom. Mamori scowled.

Three days later, they returned to the game world the same way they'd first traveled there. Seeing the fake brown buildings and wasteland and smelling the dirt as it filled her nose, it truly felt like Shadow Gale had returned to the same place. Opening the map, she noted the locations of her party members and made to meet up with Kanoe first.

"Well, you certainly kept me waiting," said Pfle. "Come to me faster next time."

"Yes, yes," Shadow Gale replied. "I'll run to you as fast as I can."

Masked Wonder seemed to be trapped in an area a little ways away. She was a real weirdo, but still, she wasn't two-faced like Pfle, and she kind of felt easier to hang out with. The icon displaying Masked Wonder's location was stuck on one spot. They'd agreed to meet up with one another once they were back in the game, but Masked Wonder seemed to be waiting for them to come to her.

Pfle, who had needled Shadow Gale for being late, didn't say a thing about Masked Wonder just standing there. But thanks to her observation of the Hitokouji family for over ten years, Mamori understood why. Investors were lenient with talented personnel. They always got priority treatment when it came to pay, care, and hours. The less talented, on the other hand, got the short end of the stick.

With great effort, Shadow Gale pushed Pfle's wheelchair until they arrived in front of the building where Masked Wonder was waiting for them. Shadow Gale stretched her back and felt a slight chill there. She was sweating.

Was Masked Wonder preparing to do her stupid "victory pose" again? Irritated, Shadow Gale pushed open the door and saw her lying there. Her arms were stretched in front of her, as if reaching out for something. She was on her stomach, facedown, dark-red fluid staining her purple cape. The red-black wasn't just dirtying the cape—it was spread out all over the floor, too. The flow originated from the back of Masked Wonder's head, mercilessly crushed underneath a large rock.

Pfle rolled her wheelchair through the puddle of blood toward the dead girl, bent over, and scooped up her magical phone. She turned it on.

"Hmm…shoot. All her items and candy were taken." Pfle spoke as if she were discussing how she'd guessed an answer on a test and gotten it wrong.

Shadow Gale listened in a daze, but nausea threatened to surface like a memory.

☆ Pechka

She'd gotten herself a pot.

The shop stocks varied by town: The wasteland shop carried recovery items, while the mountain shop had encyclopedias. Each shop also provided weapons and armor that were more powerful than those in the previous area. The wasteland store sold plain weapon and shield equipment, the grasslands shop had "weapon +1" and "shield +1" items, and at the mountain shop, there were +2 items. After installing a purchase, you could summon it, and each upgrade was more durable and looked more refined than the last. The weapons also varied depending on which magical girl summoned it, so putting one in Pechka's phone produced a spatula, but Rionetta's produced claws. The naming scheme "weapon +X" was bland, but flexible.

The only items a party could share were the random results of R and the special passes. R had been extremely popular at the beginning of the game. The first item Pechka's party had gotten from it, the map, was so useful that the price of one hundred candy was totally worth it if all the drops were of the same caliber—or so they believed. But reality is never so kind, even in a game.

The second time they bought an R, they rolled another map. The third time, a map. The fourth time, a map. They'd been laughing it off up until the third one. The fourth made their smiles vanish. The fifth incited anger and suspicion. What the hell was up with this R item? Did it only drop maps?

"R generates items of differing rarities, and the probability of receiving any given item varies, pon." Upon being summoned via the HELP button, Fal responded dispassionately and unflinchingly to their barrage of anger.

"We've only ever received maps, though." Rionetta's voice was shaking, and the corners of her lips were drawn tight.

But Fal was the same as ever. "The map is an extremely common item, pon. It's normal for it to drop four or even five times in a row. But please just shake it off and roll again and again to try for a super-rare item, pon."

Brandishing the map with beautiful and experienced form, Rionetta flung it against the wall. A message appeared:

This item sells for 3 candy.

After that, their party leader forbade them from purchasing any more *R*. The goblins that populated the mountain area dropped lots of candy, and the items in the shop were generally cheap anyway, so their candy stores grew and grew.

But Nonako Miyokata pestered them with "I want to buy an *R*, I want to buy an *R*" until eventually Clantail allowed it. The other three didn't want any weapons, so Clantail had been using their candy to purchase armaments for herself. Now she wielded a long assault spear in her right hand and a large shield in her left. Perhaps she felt she shouldn't be so stingy now, and that was why she couldn't refuse Nonako's request.

Rionetta still had reservations but ultimately agreed, so they spent one thousand candy on ten *R* and ended up with eight maps, one shovel, and one pot. The shovel was as ordinary as could be, about three feet long. The cookware, too, was a normal stockpot. Neither had any magical properties or unique effects.

At this point, Rionetta was furious. She wailed and called Nonako an idiot for spending a thousand candy on junk. Nonako snapped back at her for the insult. This turned into an argument, which Clantail attempted to break up, but neither of them listened to her, and their unproductive squabble continued until the fighting and scouting parties each went their separate ways.

Nonako Miyokata's bad mood soon abated. As they explored, she mowed down every enemy they crossed, while Pechka ran away, avoiding them. Nonako purified a goblin and made it into her familiar, squealing over how cute it was. She even tied a bow around its neck. Back when it had been attacking them, it had seemed so creepy, but now that it was attached to Nonako...well, it could pass for cute, even if it looked exactly the same. Seeing them together was kind of heartwarming.

Rionetta's mood, on the other hand, only worsened.

At night, they met back up with the combat party, but neither Clantail nor Rionetta would speak. They were so quiet, the sound of Clantail's hooves clopping on the ground was deafening by comparison. Any eye contact with her elicited a screech of "What in the hell was that about?!" that made her anger clear. "What is that giant rat constantly blocking our path?!"

That "giant rat" had chased them away once before with a warning to stay away from their group's hunting ground. Apparently, she'd done it again once Clantail and Rionetta had moved on to the mountain area.

Rionetta was so angry she snapped at everything in sight. When she spotted Nonako Miyokata's tamed goblin, her eyes went narrow, and she shrieked, "Don't you dare allow that thing near me! I don't want its dirty smell on me!" and that sparked another shouting match until Clantail intervened.

Then Rionetta's eyes rested on Pechka. "What are you doing?" she asked.

"Um...the pot..."

"I was already quite cross that we squandered so much candy on that thing. I'd really rather you not force me to look at it any longer. Just remembering how we spent a thousand candy to get *that* and a spade will keep me awake at night." Hunger was part of the game mechanics, but sleep wasn't. In other words, her complaints of insomnia were complete nonsense.

"What's with that queer pose, anyway? And why are you sticking your hands in the pot—huh?" Rionetta's nose twitched. She sniffed and looked at the pot.

A stiff smile spread across Pechka's face as she timidly fumbled to explain. "My magic, it's, um... As I explained before...I can make nice meals. So, since we have a pot now...maybe we wouldn't have to rely on rations... And I'm not using my candy... I can make food... without any ingredients at all...so, well...I think... I think it should taste...better than the rations..."

"Well, aren't you confident in yourself?" said Rionetta.

"Not really... Um, we don't have any utensils, so... I'm sorry, but you'll have to make do with leaves..."

"Leaves! What a wonderfully rustic utensil!"

"If you're going to complain about it, you don't have to eat it, *je crois*." Nonako Miyokata laughed, and her goblin chuckled and hopped about. Rionetta clicked her tongue, thoroughly irked, and plopped down on a nearby rock, where she purposefully kicked up dirt.

If Pechka put her mind to it, she could make the fanciest dish in the world. But if she were to serve a fancy dish outdoors on big leaves, she'd just be inviting a pile of complaints. *"It's too hard to dish out! It's too hard to eat!"* they'd say. So instead, she had come up with a simple, easy-to-eat meal that would place emphasis on the good taste of fresh food.

"Rice balls? After all that prating, you give us rice balls?" Rionetta insulted Pechka's cooking on sight. "Why should I eat this peasant food? I'd rather eat rations," she spat. Then she took a bite. Her brows came together.

Clantail and Nonako watched her with some suspicion. Ignoring their gaze, Rionetta took a second bite, then a third. She devoured the whole thing. Then she grabbed another without comment and chowed down on it.

Cautiously, Nonako took a bite of a rice ball. "Oh…" She voiced her surprise quietly, and then she began devouring the food, just like Rionetta. The goblin, seeing its master so excited, gobbled one down, too. Clantail was the only one who ate with even an ounce of poise, but her tail was wagging from side to side.

For now, everyone seemed to be enjoying the food. Pechka breathed a sigh of relief and began eating a rice ball.

She'd done the same thing once, long ago. She couldn't remember very well, but she was sure something like this had happened before. Pechka had cooked a meal with her magic in an attempt to get a group of people to get along. But it couldn't have been that long ago. It had happened once she'd become a magical girl, so there should be no reason she wouldn't remember. Why couldn't she recall it?

Rionetta, Nonako, and Clantail were all focused on stuffing

their cheeks with rice balls. Only moments ago, they'd been so angry at being body-blocked out of a hunting ground, but now they were entirely focused on eating. Her magic, which Pechka had only ever considered secondary to her looks, had allowed her to approach Ninomiya and had even cheered up her party members. *Maybe cooking is worth something*, she thought.

☆ **Nokko**

Fourth year, class two at Manabegawa Elementary No. 3 was a "good class."

On sports day and during cultural festivals, the whole class worked together as a group—but when people screwed up during these events, they were never scorned or belittled. If they did well, the whole class shared in the joy, and even if they didn't, they were still all able to smile about it.

The class didn't have any of the common social problems, like conflict between the boys and the girls, bullying of the weak, or nasty rumors going around.

Their teacher was Mr. Noguchi, who had taught sixth grade up until the previous year. He was famously short-tempered, quick to yell at students, and he had been nicknamed "the Square Teakettle" for the shape of his face. But this Mr. Noguchi, ever since transferring to class 4-2, had transformed into an entirely different person: the brightest, most fun teacher ever. He'd never yelled at a single child all year.

Why was class 4-2 such a pleasant place? Only Noriko Nonohara knew the answer.

If someone was upset, she would crank up their joy. If someone was sad, she would turn down their emotional fragility. Anger, jealousy, nastiness—everything unnecessary for a good class, she suppressed, manipulating the students to create a fun and bright class. By using her magical ability to transmit her emotions to those around her, the magical girl Nokko could unify her class from the shadows.

Noriko Nonohara was a hard-core magical girl. How so? Because from birth to the present day, the time she'd spent as a magical girl far exceeded her time spent as a normal person. She'd become Nokko at age four and was now ten, so that was six years of magical-girl experience. She was a veteran among veterans.

The question of how to live as a magical girl was a matter of philosophy, and Nokko knew the easiest shortcuts. Though "easiest shortcuts" didn't simply mean skipping out on school or shirking responsibilities. She knew shortcuts that brand-new magical girls couldn't possibly be aware of.

The Magical Kingdom was incapable of adapting. It was stubborn and bullheaded, and it never backed down on its decisions. Perhaps that made it rather similar to human governments. Everything Nokko had told Magical Daisy about how Noriko had become Nokko was true.

But for all the Magical Kingdom's stubbornness, it was comparatively lax with security. The region Nokko was charged with was managed through an experimental system whereby a leader-like magical girl kept watch over a number of other magical girls, reporting to the Magical Kingdom and acting as an intermediary. The Magical Kingdom didn't observe or direct the magical girls' activities directly, so they had to rely heavily on the supervisor's discretion to enforce rules. If she was lazy, stupid, unruly, selfish, an anomaly, or didn't care about obeying the rules, then she would be unlikely to report others for their lack of diligence.

The leader of Nokko's group was the type not to report them no matter what they did, so Nokko was never admonished for using her abilities to improve her own life instead of helping others. Maintaining a low profile, she used her magic to solve problems on the sly. After school, she would visit her mother in the hospital and help ease her depression. Then she would go home and spend all her time doing chores.

Nokko's magic didn't allow her to control others' emotions at will. She could only transmit her own emotions to them. If she wanted to make someone excited, she needed to focus hard on something she had once found exciting and then remember, remember, remember, until her magic finally worked.

As a result, she became an expert in fooling herself by the young age of ten. Since her mother was in the hospital, Noriko was in charge of housework. This was exhausting. She had no time to go out and use her magic to make the world a better place. Her hands were already full taking care of herself. But even so, she'd managed. At least, so far.

Six months earlier, Nokko's superior—the leader magical girl—had been permanently expelled. Some unforgivable acts she'd committed had come to light. The Magical Kingdom had immediately dispatched a replacement, not wanting to believe that a magical girl, the symbol of hopes and dreams, could be a rotten apple. After that, the new girl served her role as leader with great enthusiasm. But the fact that she was picking up after someone who had been dismissed due to scandal meant that she was overly serious and inflexible, like a manifestation of the Magical Kingdom itself.

So on top of everything else, Noriko found herself required to complete her magical-girl duty of helping others. There was a real possibility of that stick-up-her-butt leader delivering a report: *She only ever thinks of herself! She isn't actually doing her job!* At worst, it might even lead to her losing her status as a magical girl.

So Noriko now had to shepherd her class, help people in town, do chores, *and* participate in the game. She had no interest in the game itself and didn't have time to help future magical girls, but the participation and completion rewards were mighty attractive. If she could get her hands on ten million yen, a sum she'd never even seen before, then she'd put in some effort to complete the virtual tasks.

Noriko looked at her bank account again. For more than six months, it hadn't seen a single deposit. Now there was a hundred thousand yen sitting in it. And if she could open up a new area, that was another million yen.

Genopsyko's helmet bubbled up to the lava's surface. Then her visor, neck, and hands appeared, and a small key was in her grasp.

@Meow-Meow, who had been holding her breath next to Nokko, let out a big sigh of relief.

"Found it!" announced Genopsyko. "There was an altar thing at the bottom, just like the ancient text described! It was right inside that! Man, I had to feel around for the thing, and it took a hell of a long time."

"Yumenoshima, I thought you melt," said @Meow-Meow.

"Nah, I'm not gonna melt. I told ya, this suit could take even the Big Bang!" Genopsyko grabbed hold of the cliff and hauled herself onto land. Just as she'd said, her suit wasn't melted or burned at all. Genopsyko herself didn't seem to be hurt, either. Scraping off the lava clinging to her, she lifted her visor and flashed a smile. "Gate key and one million yen, in the bag! Now we can head to the next area!" The area following the grasslands, the mountain area, was already unlocked when they'd logged back in. Some party had apparently done it right before logging out the last time.

The hordes of goblins, equipped with short spears, daggers, short bows, javelins, small shields, and leather armor, had slightly more brute strength and tactical organization than the skeletons. Some of the goblins wore dirty robes and wielded crooked staffs, and they would mutter mysterious chants to summon and launch fireballs the size of human heads. Goblins double the size of normal ones also accompanied these hordes, swinging clubs with all their might—a might which rivaled even a magical girl's.

Even so, these goblins were no match for them, mostly with regard to speed and ability to take a hit. For every one movement a goblin made, a magical girl could make ten. And the monsters' attacks hurt, but that was all. Similar attacks from the girls would leave their enemies with fatal wounds. Unlike the skeletons, though, the goblins bled, and this encounter with their biology was revolting. Seeing their jaws full of crooked teeth being crushed, white enamel and blood flying through the air, made Nokko feel sick. Smashing a skeleton's skull was nowhere near as visceral as smashing a goblin's skull with her mop. She really felt like she was taking a life. The corpses would disappear after two hours, but the sensation remained. There was such a thing as being too real.

On top of all this, Nokko still wasn't over the shock of Magical Daisy's death. But she couldn't play this game if she was going to feel such disgust over killing every single monster. So Nokko focused entirely on distracting herself, filling her mind with happy, fun thoughts to support Genopsyko and @Meow-Meow.

Magical Daisy's death had been an accident. No one was responsible. Nokko knew that if she started thinking about what-ifs, like what if Daisy had been more careful when confronting an unknown enemy, or what if they'd bought a monster encyclopedia before going out to battle, she'd never stop. Still, she couldn't forget the brutal image of Daisy bleeding out from the gaping hole in her body. Most likely, it would never leave her memory. Nor would she forget digging a hole and burying Daisy's body in it, then setting a stone on it in place of a grave marker as the three of them cried and hugged each other.

But that was an accident. Genopsyko liked to mention that Daisy wasn't dead in the real world or anything, as if trying to convince herself that was true. And Nokko wanted her to think like that. That was how she *should* be thinking. And Nokko could help her party with that.

They couldn't stay sad forever. Even if the game wasn't real, the players needed to forget their sadness and focus on completing it. Nokko also threw her whole self into the task.

Upon entering the mountain area, they had come across a run-down shack. Inside, they discovered a book labeled ANCIENT TEXT. The title was no lie. From annotations to postscript, it was all written in a mysterious language.

So they purchased the app Translator Buddy in the mountain shop and deciphered the document. They had to obtain the staff of the mountain people and use that to perform their community's ritual in their temple, granting them the mark of the mountain people. With it, they would proceed to the lake of lava and perform their folk dance, causing the altar to appear. Within it lay the key of the mountain people, which would let them access the next area. Also, as an addendum: They would learn the dance by placing the hookah of the mountain people upon the scales in the village, which would then unlock the instructions in their phones. The hookah itself would be assembled from three pieces, each of which could only be found by discovering the corresponding clues to their locations.

Once they were done reading about that long, tedious process, Genopsyko's right arm shot into the air. "If it's just lava, that's easy!" she announced, and dropping her helmet's visor and sweeping aside nervous hands from Nokko and @Meow-Meow, she dove into the lake of lava. She took her time reaching the bottom and grabbed the key.

"Man, Genopsyko, you're practically cheating!" Genopsyko praised herself. "God-level skills, man, seriously god-level. A million yen! I'm so stoked! Why don't we meet up offline after and spend some of this on a party?"

"Oh, a party sounds nice."

"Yeah, how many time you get to drink one million yen for free?"

"Whoa, whoa, whoa! @Meow-Meow, you're gonna blow it all on booze? At least save some! Money's precious!"

Suddenly, the sulfuric stink and burning heat of a molten lake they'd rather have escaped as soon as possible belonged to the site of a wondrous memory. Chatting and hugging, the three of them laughed for the first time since Magical Daisy's passing. Nokko transmitted the joy she was feeling into the others.

"Now we can move on to next area. Unlock area mean candy reward."

"Oh, you're right! We just got five hundred more candy!! Woohoo!" cheered Genopsyko.

"Then first," said Nokko, "we should return to the mountain town..."

Then all their phones sounded the text-alert noise. When they checked, they found the HELP buttons on their phones were flashing.

"This is an emergency summons, pon. Everyone, please gather in the square in the wasteland town, pon."

Genopsyko tapped her helmet with a fingertip, then hurriedly snatched it away. Nokko assumed she had tried to scratch her head but the helmet got in the way. "You caught us right when we were having a good time, though," Genopsyko said.

"This is very urgent, pon. You will all be teleported here in one minute, pon. Thank you, and see you soon, pon." The black-and-white sphere, having delivered its message, disappeared. With no one to protest against, the girls had no choice but to obey.

"Well, looks like something's happened," said Nokko. "Let's go and see."

"That furry creep shows up at the worst times," moaned Genopsyko.

"I hope it nothing bad."

@Meow-Meow looked worried, and Genopsyko was clearly irritated. Nokko's only choice was to think fun and happy thoughts.

☆ Pechka

"All right, Fal has a few corrections and announcements to make, pon."

The square was once again full of magical girls, just as it had been the other day. Some were sitting on the fountain edge, while others leaned against the walls of buildings. It was quite the spectacle, even though Pechka had already seen it once before.

The atmosphere among their party had changed considerably since Fal's message around noon. It had been about a day since Pechka had first cooked for the others, and since then, she'd also created two more meals. With her magic, she could make the fanciest dish in only five minutes. Making a full-course meal took no longer than heating a microwavable snack. And no matter what she made, they loved it.

Nonako Miyokata and Rionetta would praise her endlessly, each trying to outdo the other, and while Clantail's mouth stayed taciturnly shut, her tail wagged happily from side to side.

"*Délicieux!* Pechka, this is amazing!" said Nonako.

"Exquisite flavor," Rionetta agreed. "I would even accept you as my personal chef."

Their change in attitude persisted even outside of mealtimes. They offered to do physical labor for her, prioritized her when distributing items, and did all sorts of other kindnesses. No one had further complaints about Pechka avoiding fights, not even Rionetta, who'd been so sarcastic about it.

"Just imagine if something were to happen, and your hands were injured in battle. You wouldn't be able to create food anymore! That would be a loss not only for our party, but for the entire world." Rionetta laid on the praise, eyes brimming with emotion as she clasped Pechka's hands gently.

Now Pechka could be confident. She wasn't useless anymore. They all needed her.

The other parties seemed fairly content as well, aside from one. The girl in the black nurse outfit was shaking, her face pale. *She must be suffering, too,* Pechka thought, concerned for her, though they'd never exchanged words.

"Let's start with the corrections," Fal began. Sand filled center of the fountain, and there was a magical phone fixed there from which Fal's hologram was projected. The air in this place hung heavy with dust, of which the hologram illuminated every tiny speck.

"There was a difference of opinion between Fal and Fal's master regarding damage feedback, pon. In terms of basic damage, your bodies will not be affected. Cut flesh and broken bones won't reflect on your real body. But if you happen to die, your heart will receive a significant shock, pon. This is the unavoidable effect of a realistic experience of something as traumatic to a living creature as death—even though it's a virtual world, pon. I hope you will please forgive us, pon. In addition, this is a very secret game, pon. If you talk to any outsiders about it, you will receive a punishment tantamount to in-game death, so please be careful, pon. And that's all the additional information I have for today, pon."

All sounds in the square disappeared except for the wind carrying the sand and dust. Everyone was staring at Fal, considering the meaning of what it had just said in silence. They were all speechless.

The first to speak up was a magical girl who was covered in blue. "Is this a joke?"

"No," Fal replied. "From now on, I'll only tell you the truth, pon. If you want to survive, please work to complete the game, pon. Even if you do perish, you can rest assured that your promised reward will be deposited into your account."

"That's bullshit!"

"What the hell are you saying?"

"You think we'll accept that?"

Angry shouts flew around incessantly.

Fal, emotionless as ever, took it all without flinching. "This is essentially a selection test, pon. You are being tested on whether you deserve to be magical girls, pon. If you do, you can complete the game. If you want to survive this, work to complete the game, pon. As long as you can finish the game, you will survive, pon," he repeated. "That is the message from Fal's master." Fal finished by informing them this was a decision from someone on high and was not up for discussion.

Pechka was shivering. She wanted to run, but she had nowhere to go. The blood was draining from her head. Her legs felt weak, like she could fall over at any moment. But she didn't.

The girls yelled, screamed, punched walls, and tried to grab Fal, but they only ended up swiping at the air. Static noise filled the hologram, but they couldn't touch the mascot.

"I have a few questions, if I may?" That was the girl in the wheelchair, Pfle. She was as calm as Pechka remembered her being during their last meeting, back in the grasslands town. Her steady voice carried through the chaos, silencing the yelling and screaming. Everyone looked at her.

Pfle addressed Fal. "About how you said we'd receive a significant shock to our hearts—is it possible to survive this?"

"No, pon. Certainly not as a human, and not even transforming into a magical girl would help."

"What would happen if there was an attempt to resuscitate?"

"It wouldn't work, pon."

"You could at least have left us one way out… Well then, if you know the reason our phones are malfunctioning, I'd like to hear it. You're the ones preventing us from contacting the Magical Kingdom, aren't you?"

A murmur ran through the crowd. It was true: They hadn't been able to contact the Magical Kingdom. Pechka had tried to contact them concerning the game, but no matter how many messages she sent, they had all bounced back. She should have found it strange, but she'd just figured that this sort of thing happened sometimes. It couldn't have been solely because her head was full of thoughts of Ninomiya.

Fal blinked. "You're not allowed to tell anyone about this game, so I think it's actually a good thing that you can't contact the Magical Kingdom, pon."

"A good thing, huh?" Pfle murmured. Then she spread her arms wide and spoke loudly. Maintaining the projection, pitch, and beauty of her voice, she sermonized in a resounding tone that dispelled all the clamoring in the square. "It seems our overlords want us to continue this game whether we like it or not. As we can see from their ability to teleport us at will, they have the power to do anything they want with us."

"We're not gonna give in to someone like that!" the girl in the hamster suit yelled loudly, interrupting Pfle.

Pfle glanced over at her. "We're in this situation precisely because giving in is all we can do." Then she added, "Let's continue the game."

There were many protests to this. "So we just have to accept our enemy's plan?"

"Just bow down?"

"There's no point in playing this game!"

"Shouldn't we be trying to defeat this new enemy?"

Pfle nodded at each objection but remained steadfast. "I know you all probably hate the idea of playing a game you don't understand and doing whatever this master wants you to do while being completely cut off from the Magical Kingdom. But the fact that this individual can force a bunch of magical girls to play along means they're easily capable of much more. We may want to defeat this enemy, but as long as we are in the palm of their hand, it shouldn't be our goal. For now, let's just do what we're told."

"But even if we do complete the game, there's no real guarantee we'll be released, is there?" That was Rionetta. Naturally, she was angry.

"It sounds crazy, I'm aware, but we have no choice but to trust this 'master.' I received a reward deposited into my account the other day. I'm sure others among you have confirmed your own deposits. So it seems they at least are intent on paying us. Though it's just a conciliatory amount."

"I'll admit that the reward is attractive," said Rionetta. "But didn't we all agree to play this game on the basis that dying would cause us no harm?"

"Regarding that," Fal interjected, drawing all eyes. Everyone was glaring daggers at the mascot. "There will be no lies or trickery from here on out, pon. Fal's words are the master's words. It's all true, pon."

"And I'm asking how we can be sure of that," said Rionetta.

"Fal can only tell you to please have faith, pon."

"They don't need proof. If they tell us to do something, we have no choice but to obey. We're birds in a cage." Pfle's choice of words seemed almost defeatist, but Pechka couldn't detect any resignation in her tone. Her expression was so alive, it was eerie.

"May I ask something as well?" Another girl stood up, raising her right hand. She was wearing a deerstalker cap along with a cape and a coat, like a private eye. "I'm Detec Bell. I may not look it, but I'm actually a detective." She clearly did look the part, so perhaps that was a joke meant to try to ease the tension. Maybe. But no one was laughing, and no one even attempted to point out the discrepancy.

Detec Bell continued. "The other day, immediately after being released from the game, I spent some time investigating the whereabouts of a certain individual. Their situation is extremely pertinent to what's going on here."

"Bell, you're really primin' for a dramatic reveal, here. Who're you talkin' about?" the blue magical girl asked.

Detec Bell closed her eyes. "I'm talking about Magical Daisy. I've been investigating her in the real world." Opening her eyes, she continued. "Some of you may know about her. Her past exploits as a magical girl were the basis for a TV anime. So I set out to the neighborhood the anime was set in, using my magic to uncover the facts. Magical Daisy did, in fact, operate there at one time. So I investigated further, using my magic to track down her current location. I discovered her family's home, then headed to her apartment from there. The building was surrounded by police cars, an ambulance, and a crowd. I asked around, and her time of death was during the time in the game world...which was just an instant in the real world, wasn't it? It was essentially that very instant."

Magical Daisy was dead. This backed up Fal's statement that an in-game demise meant real-world death as well.

"Magical Daisy was quite famous," Detec Bell went on. "Her sudden death could tip off the Magical Kingdom that something strange is going on. So perhaps now that they're exposed, they can't continue to hide the fact that in-game deaths will be linked to the real world as they force us to play." Detec Bell looked at Fal, who bobbed in the air.

"You may interpret it that way, pon."

Detec Bell nodded in satisfaction. "That's all from me."

She returned to her original position and sat down. The blue magical girl was clamoring, "Bell, that was amazing! You really are a super detective!"

But Pechka had to wonder if she truly grasped the situation. Those who did all seemed disturbed. Clantail was tapping her hooves, her tail between her legs. Nonako Miyokata's face was half-angry, half-crying as she fiddled with her yin-yang ornaments.

Rionetta was clearly furious. "Oh, for crying out loud! Just what have we gotten into?"

"*Je* can't believe this...," Nonako muttered. They were all, in their own ways, reacting to the terrible news.

But it all seemed so empty to Pechka. Did they really understand the gravity of the situation? They'd all probably been sort of
thinking that things might turn out like this. Every word out of
their mouths sounded to her like lines read from a script. It seemed
like she'd heard it all before.

"*Mais* Detec Bell said it, too...," said Nonako. "Magical Daisy
has clearly died in the real world."

"She could be a spy sent by the master simply to support Fal's
story," Rionetta suggested.

"*Maaais*, it just doesn't seem like—"

"I'm *trying* to tell you that we can't trust anyone!"

"May I add one more thing?" It was Pfle again. She'd changed
places with Detec Bell and was sitting alone next to the mermaid
statue. "This may not be something I should really be saying at a
time like this...but if we don't take care of this now, it could get
much worse." Her eyes met Pechka's, and for some reason, she
smiled. Pechka jerked her gaze away. What must be going on in her
head right now for her to manage a smile?

"I propose we work together!" Pfle announced, her voice loud
and clear. All eyes gathered on her. She continued, decisive. "After
we logged back in, in the few moments before our party could find
one another again, someone killed one of ours, Masked Wonder!
If death in reality and this realm are linked, then this means she
really is dead." Her final words were like a whisper. "All of her
items and candy, including the item we earned from the event
before we logged out last time, were stolen! I ask that the criminal
name themselves!"

"No way!" the blue magical girl shouted. "Comrade Wonder
was super-strong! There's no way she'd get killed that easy!"

"In a game full of magical girls, mere strength is no guarantee
of survival," Pfle stated.

Unable to refute that, the blue-clad girl's face twisted, and her
head drooped. Balling her fists tight, she quaked quietly. Detec Bell
put a hand on her shoulder and said something to her. Probably
comforting her, Pechka thought.

The crowd buzzed. It was only natural. Not only had Fal dropped a bomb on them, but here came another one out of nowhere amid all the chaos.

"So it wasn't a monster that killed her?" Rionetta expressed her doubts, and Pechka sympathized entirely. Even without bringing up Magical Daisy's fate, it was natural to assume that it would be the game's enemies doing players harm.

"The only monsters we encountered in the wasteland were regular skeletons," said Pfle. "I assure you personally, she was not the sort to be done in by such weaklings. Also…are there any here who were partied with Magical Daisy?"

A girl in a maid outfit who appeared to be about ten years old shakily raised her hand.

Pfle turned to her. "What happened to Magical Daisy's items and candy?"

"Um…well…uh…some of it, we spent on the funeral. The rest…well…we, uh, discussed it, and decided to share it…" She spoke hesitantly, as if it were difficult to say. Of course—anyone would find that awkward to confess. Some people might certainly interpret their actions in the nastiest light and judge them to be grave robbers. After answering, the small girl made herself even smaller and hid behind the girl in the cheongsam.

"Did you hear that?" Pfle turned her right palm upward and traced an arc with her hand. "Dying to the monsters doesn't make your items or candy disappear from your magical phones! But Masked Wonder's phone was devoid of both! Is this not the ultimate proof that they were stolen?"

Rionetta, Clantail, Nonako Miyokata, and Pechka all looked at each other. They'd been teleported into the game with no say in the matter, so everyone had to have appeared at the same time. Their party had met up as soon as possible without stopping to do any side quests. Had there even been time for someone to commit murder and steal the victim's items? Obviously, Pechka hadn't done it, and she doubted the other three would have had the time to do so, either. At the very least, it seemed the murderer wasn't among their party.

"I ask that the murderer be honest and name themselves!" Pfle continued. "Right after logging in, you couldn't have known that in-game deaths would be lethal in the real world! Masked Wonder died because of this game! I will not blame you for it! Just come forth!"

Nobody moved. Whispers filled the air.

Pfle took out her magical phone. "Then show me proof. The murderer will have Masked Wonder's Miracle Coin in their phone."

More whispering. At length, Clantail sighed and stepped forward. "What's the point in looking now? Are you trying to start a witch hunt?"

"I suppose 'witch' is not an inaccurate term for us. Clever."

Clantail glared daggers at her for the crack.

Pfle cleared her throat and changed the subject. "It's no great concern if some magical girl who's usually a paragon of good conduct indulges in something naughty in a game, like this player kill. If she names herself and comes forth, we can just call it an unfortunate episode...but I do want the Miracle Coin back. If no one confesses, then I have reason to worry."

"About what?" Clantail demanded.

"That there may be a wolf in sheep's clothing among us. We can't rule out the possibility that one of the magical girls here is carrying out the master's will."

Clantail said nothing.

Pfle took it even further. "She might not even be a spy. The mastermind could be among us. Did I get that right?" she asked Fal, but the mascot said nothing. It just floated there in silence. "Fal says he will speak only the truth, and now it seems he doesn't want to reply. That just makes me all the more anxious to dispel our worries. So, first of all, is anyone willing to step forth?"

Every one of them kept their mouths shut.

"Then show me your magical phones," Pfle ordered. "If you're just a victim, merely one of the poor magical girls forced into this game, then you should have no problem showing us your item bank."

Clantail spat on the ground and glared at Pfle. The flash in her eyes would have started Pechka crying instantly, but Pfle met her gaze head-on, her expression relaxed. Clantail flung her phone at her, and Pfle caught it with one hand.

The crowd hushed as everyone watched the pair's exchange.

"Thank you. I appreciate this." Pfle checked the phone. "Nope, no problem here. No Miracle Coin in your bank. Just to be safe, will you check my phone as well?" She handed Clantail's phone back while also offering her own.

Silently, Clantail took it. "…Nothing suspicious." She practically shoved it back into Pfle's hands.

"Now, if everyone else would please cooperate. The only person who has reason to worry is the murderer. If you're innocent, you shouldn't have any reason to hesitate."

A number of people complained, "Why are we under investigation?" and "Is she even telling the truth?" But it seemed everyone—including Pechka—arrived at the conclusion that it was better than being suspected. They lined up to have Pfle check their phones. From the moment she offered her phone until she got it back, Pechka was incredibly nervous, even though she couldn't possibly be the murderer.

As Clantail had checked Pfle's phone, she had also inspected the one belonging to Pfle's companion, the nurse. *Why would someone want to check the phones of those in Masked Wonder's party, too?* Pechka wondered, but then she quickly realized either of the two could have snatched all of Masked Wonder's items while nonchalantly declaring that they had been stolen. It chilled Pechka to realize she was thinking like this.

Now that each phone had been searched, the line in front of Pfle dispersed. Everyone returned to their original positions, and Pfle called out to a certain corner of the square, "All right. I've checked everyone but you. If you aren't the murderer, then I ask that you cooperate with us."

Pechka looked to see who it was and was startled. It was a girl in a samurai-esque outfit, a naked Japanese blade dangling from her right hand. She remembered that girl. There was no way she could forget. She was the one Pechka had encountered at the beginning of the game. She'd wiped out the skeletons and proceeded to nearly strangle Pechka to death.

"Come," Pfle pressed her, but the samurai girl didn't move. She at least appeared to have heard, since her eyes were locked on the girl in the wheelchair. The sword at her side swayed.

"Hurry up, now. Everyone's waiting."

Pechka could have sworn she could hear the air creaking with the pressure. She swallowed. It was possible everyone was thinking the same thing she was. They had checked every other magical phone but this one, and the stolen item hadn't been in any of them. In other words, the last person remaining had to have it, right?

Pfle kept her hand outstretched, but the girl refused to move. Everyone else watched with bated breath. They didn't want to stare down some possibly unstable person with a drawn blade hanging at her side.

"Hey, hey! You there!"

To Pechka's shock, someone did step forward. She wore a helmet on her head with little protrusions on the sides that looked like cat ears. The semitransparent visor was down, hiding her face. Her near-future-style skintight suit called to mind a costume from the reruns of a special-effects-heavy show Pechka had once seen about transforming superheroes.

"Being difficult is only gonna make people more suspicious. Just accept it and show us your phone, boss." Her attitude was so confident, you wouldn't think she was addressing a questionable individual with a naked blade. The girl in the power suit reached out to place her hand on the samurai girl's shoulder, but she was swatted away.

The samurai narrowed one eye, studying the other girl. Her gaze was unrelenting. "...Are you the Musician?"

"Sorry?"

"Are you the Musician?"

"Oh, yeah, you could say I'm a musician. I actually sometimes use Vocaloids to make songs and upload them—"

The Japanese sword swung through empty air, followed by a

soft slap like the sound of a wet rag. The inside of the suited girl's visor splattered with red, and she crumpled to the ground.

Someone screamed.

☆ Nokko

"Now, calm down." Pfle, her hand still outstretched, addressed the girl with the sword. Not a speck of blood stained the blade. It shone like silver under the intense light of the sun.

Nokko was doing her best to restrain @Meow-Meow from running over to Genopsyko. "Yumenoshima hurt! We have to…we have to help her!" @Meow-Meow cried.

"Calm down… Just calm down…"

Now was not the time to be rash. Nokko understood that @Meow-Meow was upset, but it was still a bad idea. The murderer would strike again if provoked. If anyone moved, someone was sure to die, and it would be the one who provoked her. Calming herself, Nokko transferred her serenity to @Meow-Meow. But even so, she avoided looking at Genopsyko.

"Why don't you put down that blade first? We can talk this out once you abandon the weapon." Pfle was smiling like she hadn't just witnessed a death. Evenly, she pressed for surrender, as simultaneously, a ray of light shot out and then split in two. The dark-clad nurse flew forward, tackling Pfle. A giant slice appeared in the ground where Pfle had been just moments ago.

Nokko was a veteran. She'd seen plenty of fights between magical girls, so she had a certain amount of skill in analyzing confusing fights like this.

Pfle had taken the initiative, firing a ray of light from the little bird decoration on her wheelchair, and the samurai girl had cut it in half with a swing of her sword. She followed it up with a counterattack, but the dark-clad nurse at Pfle's side had jumped in and saved her comrade.

As Nokko analyzed what had happened to this point, she was hiding in the shadow of a building. The other magical girls had also slipped behind walls and into the enemy's blind spots. Some were also striking back, while others were just trying to get away.

Several large harpoons shot through the air, but the samurai girl cut down every last one. They were sliced, split, and smacked down. Vertically, horizontally, diagonally—all of them thudded to the ground before they hit their target.

The girl with the katana hadn't moved from her original position, yet she'd still managed to destroy all those spears. When giant sunflower seeds flew at her, they too were cleaved in half, and when rocks hurtled her way, they all shattered before they fell.

Her power had to be a long-range slicing attack. Genopsyko, in her invincible suit, had been cut behind her visor. Her suit itself was undamaged, but the girl inside was bleeding profusely. In other words, this girl could probably cut anything within her field of vision. So since she'd been able to see Genopsyko's face through the translucent covering, she must have been able to cut her face. Nokko could puzzle that much out, but there was nothing she could do about it. Basically, if she stepped out of hiding, she'd be struck down.

The girl behind the building with her was hugging her knees and shivering, her white hat about to fall from her head. Nokko probably couldn't expect anything from her. There had to be other girls taking cover nearby, too, but Nokko couldn't see them from her position.

Sounds of fighting ceased from both sides, and a few minutes passed—though Nokko was judging by her internal clock, so it might actually have been less. The square was silent, and nobody moved a muscle.

Then came a great grinding sound like stone and concrete rubbing together. Slowly, it grew louder. Nokko abruptly raised her head to see that the building protecting her was about to topple on her. Not the whole structure, though—just the top half. The twenty-yard-square mass had been severed at a diagonal angle, and the upper slice was sliding down toward them. Not even a magical girl could survive unscathed if crushed under that. Nokko kicked the other girl out of the way, using the recoil to propel herself in the other direction. This should get her away from the falling concrete and also help the other girl escape—probably.

The upper half of the building slammed into the ground. Crash after crash assaulted her eardrums. The impact was so strong, the surrounding buildings visibly wobbled, and she couldn't keep on her feet. Both hands and feet on the ground, she looked through the billowing dirt clouds to see in them a girl shouldering a Japanese sword, standing there calmly.

"Are you the Musician?" The last syllable came out with a rush of air as the samurai girl raised her sword up. Nokko was just over ten yards away. Still, the assailant swung down.

In one strike, a massive rock ten feet high was sliced into two.

"Huh?" said the samurai. The way had been clear before she'd raised her sword. Just bringing the blade down should have cleanly bisected Nokko. But the moment the samurai girl's arm moved, something had intervened. A giant boulder had fallen between Nokko and the samurai, and the stone had been sliced instead of Nokko.

"Not on my watch!" @Meow-Meow stood in front of Nokko. A total of eight slips of paper gripped between her fingers, she did the same kung fu pose she'd done before.

The two stared each other down. @Meow-Meow slid forward, letting out a deep breath. Across from her, the other girl slowly raised the tip of her katana skyward.

The moment samurai girl brought down her blade, a talisman flew. It disappeared with a small explosion, leaving behind a large boulder that fell in two pieces atop of the rubble already strewn on the ground. @Meow-Meow threw seal after seal, each branded with an @ mark. They all exploded, transforming into boulders.

The samurai girl let out a strange cry, drawing her *wakizashi* short sword with her left hand. Supporting it in a light grip using only her index and middle fingers and thumb, she twirled both blades so fast it was difficult for the eye to follow. Slicing, splitting, and smashing, the samurai girl carved every single rock into dust.

Motes of broken stone flew through the air, the fine shavings forming a white mist that obscured everything in sight.

A gust of wind blew, scattering the dust and revealing two figures facing off amid a pile of mangled lumps of rock. One was the samurai girl wielding both of her swords. The other was Nokko, mop in hand.

Nokko was standing at the ready, but that didn't mean she stood a chance. At ten yards away, she had no means of attacking, and the samurai girl had to know that, based on their exchange thus far. The samurai girl's cheeks warped, flashing white teeth. She was smiling. She knew Nokko would go down without a fight; she was mocking her. The sudden shadow over the sun, the fact that @Meow-Meow was gone—none of it registered to the samurai girl. None of the details mattered. She was simply driven by her urge to cut down every enemy in sight. Her twisted smile never disappeared until the abandoned building crushed her.

Nokko looked up to the roof of the building that had come flying from the sky. There stood @Meow-Meow, her face distorted with tears, in perfect opposition to the expression of the samurai girl, which had lasted until her demise.

If @Meow-Meow hadn't been there, Nokko would have died. @Meow-Meow had protected her with those boulders. She'd scattered her talismans, summoning barrier after barrier, all the while scaling a nearby building and leaping off the roof to summon one of the dilapidated office buildings from the wasteland. That had saved Nokko's life. She wanted to thank her protector, but the sobbing @Meow-Meow wasn't in the right state for that.

This reminded Nokko that Genopsyko had been hurt. Nokko looked to where she'd collapsed after being cut down, but she was gone. Nothing but her magical phone lay there.

MASTER SIDE #3

"Sooo, how'd it go?"

"Oh, it was just awful, pon. Everyone was crying and screaming. They tried to kill Fal, pon. Could have been turned to giblets and mincemeat if Fal hadn't been a hologram, pon."

"I see, I see." The girl's cheeks relaxed into a slight smile. Putting her left index finger to the frame of her glasses, she adjusted their position. "Still, they've somewhat accepted it, right? I think they must have known things might turn out like this, but they participated in the game anyway. No one refused; no one dragged their heels. They were just sucked into the game and accepted it." She seemed ready to make a long-winded speech, but Fal cut her off with a cough. The girl blinked twice, then looked at Fal. "What?"

"Fal has a suggestion, pon."

"Well? Go on."

"It's not too late yet, don't you think, pon?"

"Not too late for what?"

"If you turn yourself in without a struggle, maybe the Magical Kingdom will reduce your penalty, pon?"

"I doubt that."

"If you turn yourself in, at least they won't execute you, pon."

"My life isn't important. What is important is for a magical girl to *live* like one." The conversation paused there. Neither Fal nor the girl spoke for a moment.

"Fal has an idea, pon."

"What kind of idea?" The girl twirled her bangs around her fingertip. Her hair, while mostly short, had a bit of a cowlick, and she seemed particularly sensitive about how it stuck up.

"You can say Fal threatened or tricked you, pon. Or that you didn't realize Fal was acting crazy until it was too late, pon. Just blame it on Fal, pon."

"And then?"

"You turn us in, declaring that Fal was the criminal. Tell the Magical Kingdom that your sidekick decided to round up a bunch of magical girls and make them fight to the death, pon."

"Hey..." The girl turned a half circle in her revolving chair to face Fal. The momentum caused her glasses to slip down, so she once again stuck out her left middle finger to readjust them. "Do you see me as some little weakling who's trembling in fear of all she's done, a girl who simply feels she can't go back? Do I come off that *boring* to you? If your impression of me is that I'm the kind of person who would be glad to hear *'I'll take all the blame, so you go beg forgiveness'*...that's worse than disgusting. The *looowest* of the low."

"You could still—"

"You shut your mouth." The girl let go of her bangs, then immediately spun back to her original position. "Don't you throw cold water on my moral code, sidekick. Only *real* magical girls should be doing what we do. What's so wrong with that? Nothing. If you're gonna tell me that the unworthy can be magical girls, too, then the system, the tests, the Magical Kingdom, and everything else are to blame for that. And in particular, the one with the most blame to shoulder is *her.* So perhaps the second-most would be the children, right?"

The girl smiled at Fal. "I will follow my master's teachings. That's the *right* way to be a magical girl."

CHAPTER 4
MYSTERIOUS CANDY

☆ **Shadow Gale**

"Player deaths don't make items disappear," said Pfle. "So then what happens when a magical phone is destroyed? What about the items inside?"

"When a magical phone is destroyed, the items inside return to their original locations, pon. If there's an event item, that event will reactivate. Items sold in shops will be available for sale again, pon."

"Is it possible to carry around an item without installing it?"

"All items are just data and can only be materialized once installed in a magical phone, pon. All items must be installed first, whether you're looking to equip weapons and armor or use pots and cooking utensils, pon."

Since Fal had announced that death in the game equaled death in real life, making it clear that this game was illegal and unsanctioned by the Magical Kingdom, the mascot had been getting more hate than a tick or a cockroach. But Pfle had pressed the HELP button anyway and was tossing questions at the mascot as if this were the obvious course of action.

But she wasn't asking questions like *"Why are you doing all this?"* or *"Do you resent us for some reason?"* All her queries were positive in nature, those of a player looking to complete the game.

Shadow Gale was once again struck by what an abnormal human being she was. Though Masked Wonder had only worked with them for three days, she'd been their ally as they moved through the game, and her death had been brutal. To make it worse, now they knew she wasn't dead in the game alone. But Pfle showed no sign at all of shock or grieving.

The girls had offered a variety of opinions: Some had discussed how they might communicate what was going on to the Magical Kingdom, while others suggested that other magical girls could save them. None of this went anywhere, and ultimately, these proposals may not have been constructive. But wasn't it still better than dancing to the tune of the master who had forced them into this game?

Someone had suggested that the various parties should all work together, so the four leaders had had a discussion in the square. But Pfle had ended it early and gone back to Shadow Gale.

Currently, Pfle was speaking to Shadow Gale across a desk in one of the buildings on the first floor of the mountain town. This building was larger than the other houses, and Pfle could maneuver around it easily, even on her wheelchair. Also, like all the other buildings, it was empty, so no one would complain if they hung around indefinitely.

"That's all of my questions. Thank you, Fal." Pfle even included a polite expression of gratitude as she closed the HELP menu on her magical phone. The window disappeared, leaving the item confirmation screen on display. "There is one thing that's odd."

"You still haven't told me how your discussion went, though," said Shadow Gale. "What happened?"

"If I'm going to talk about that, there's something else that has to come first."

"What do you mean?"

Earlier, Fal had gathered everyone in the wasteland town square, and there, it had announced something unthinkable. Then, while all the others were restlessly worrying over what they should do, Pfle had dropped another bomb: Masked Wonder had been murdered, and all her items and candy had been stolen. Pfle had then asked the culprit to come forth.

Just recalling the vicious manner of Masked Wonder's death made Shadow Gale sick. Masked Wonder had been a weirdo, and sometimes rather pushy, but she'd still been a good person, and softhearted enough for Pfle to hook with her bandages trick. She'd been a righteous magical girl of justice who fought to protect the weak. There was no reason she had to die like that.

Pfle had told them that Masked Wonder had been mugged, meaning that whoever had the Miracle Coin had to be the culprit. *Come on,* she'd said, rushing them along. *Cooperate with me in searching for the culprit. Let me check all your magical phones, please.*

But then they'd gotten stuck on the last girl. The samurai girl had refused to show her phone, and when the suited girl had criticized her for that, the samurai had cut her up. The samurai must not have killed her—the victim had disappeared afterward. The two girls from her party were apparently looking for her, but no one had called to inform them of her location or say that they'd found her body anywhere.

The samurai had rampaged as violently as a typhoon, cutting everything in sight. She sliced and sliced and sliced to kill, even cleaving a building in two. Pfle would have died if Shadow Gale hadn't saved her. Pfle must have taken it for granted that her companion would do so, as she didn't voice a single word of gratitude. Maybe Shadow Gale should have kicked her to safety instead, if that would have worked.

Ultimately, the ruined building became the villain's tombstone. The samurai had been fighting with the girl in the Chinese dress, and then, right when she was about to kill the maid girl in front of her, a building sundered by the samurai herself had dropped on her from above to crush her. It was horrifying to know that there were so many magical girls in the world who could pull off such terrifying stunts.

The Chinese-style girl had then sealed the destroyed edifice away once more inside one of her talismans. Left in the center of the earthen pit was...the samurai girl. Shadow Gale didn't really want to recall what she'd looked like, exactly. Her magical phone had been completely unusable, the protective case broken and the LCD screen shattered, so they hadn't been able to check and see if the stolen items were on it. But since the samurai girl had refused to present her magical phone and had attacked so suddenly, and no one else had the Miracle Coin, they all just figured she must have been the culprit. So their search for the killer ended there.

After that, they all offered their opinions on what to do next and prepared for the party leaders to have a discussion. As the others occupied themselves with suggestions like *"We should do this"* or *"We should do that,"* Shadow Gale became lost in her troubles, her mind hazy.

How could all of them be so quick to get over this? Three people had died—and furthermore, they were being forced to play this game with their lives on the line. Far, far more of them should have been crying and wailing and losing their minds. Wasn't it messed up that they were all having a composed discussion about how to best deal with the situation?

All of them are trying to trick me, she thought.

When Pfle left the conversation early and came back, Shadow Gale very emphatically tried to communicate the thoughts boiling in her head.

Pfle responded, "They're not all necessarily as calm as you think they are, Mamori. Though I am."

"I know you're not bothered, miss—"

"But yes, now that you mention it, perhaps they're all relaxed about this. Look, do you remember that examiner from back when we became magical girls? Well, no matter. You know what she said.

When you become a magical girl, you don't only become stronger physically—you become strong of mind as well. Your sense of fear diminishes."

"I don't feel any less scared."

"I'm talking about the kind of ideal magical girl that the Magical Kingdom wants. The kind of saint who won't hesitate to sacrifice herself when push comes to shove. No one with a regular mentality could do that." Pfle was making sense and speaking rationally, but whether or not that would convince Shadow Gale was another issue entirely. "There's an app being sold at the shop in this town called the Item Encyclopedia. It's the item version of the monster encyclopedia that was sold at the grasslands shop." Pfle handed Shadow Gale her phone as if to say, *"Go on, take a look."* Displayed there was a long list of names. "These are the names of all the items. You can see a graphic, too, if you click on them. When you see question marks rather than an item name, it means no one has acquired the item yet. Sliding to the right, it lists how to acquire the item, how much it costs at shops, and then its use."

"What are these numbers?" asked Shadow Gale. She stared at some large numbers beside some smaller numbers in brackets. For example, to the side of the travel pass, the text read 10,000 (4). Its meaning was indecipherable from a glance.

"Good on you to have noticed that. That's important. The larger number is the upper limit for that item. The smaller one indicates how many are presently circulating in the game. With that in mind, look at this." Pfle's finger pointed to where the Miracle Coin was listed. Her finger moved to the right and then stopped at the spot where the upper limit figure and the amount in circulation were listed. There, it read 1 (1).

"So what? What does that...huh?" Shadow Gale tilted her head, confused. "The number in circulation is...one of one?"

"That's right. Strange, isn't it?" Pfle's voice held a note of enthusiasm. From the look on her face, she seemed to be enjoying herself. "When a magical phone is broken, the items within return to their original source. Any event items in there will cause the event to reactivate—that's what Fal said. If that hooligan swinging around that katana had stolen Masked Wonder's items, then when her phone was crushed by the building, the number of Miracle Coins in circulation would have turned to zero, and the event would have activated again."

"Maybe she was just carrying it around and never installed it in her phone," suggested Shadow Gale. "Or she hid it somewhere."

"That can't be done. You can't materialize an item without installing it first. I've already confirmed that fact with Fal."

"How do you know Fal isn't just lying again?"

"Fal won't lie. He's said that he'll only tell the truth from now on."

"How can you trust such a chronic liar?"

"Listen…" The enthusiasm in Pfle's voice was heating up. Her hands had been resting on the wheels of her wheelchair—but at some point, she had begun gripping the rims tight. The rubber warped, and with nowhere to go, the air within bulged out like it was about to pop. "I'm no ace detective like Detec Bell. When I seek out a culprit, I don't gather evidence or tear down alibis—though I do make inquiries, at least."

"What are you trying to say, here?"

"Fal is missing many things useful to judging his character: vocal timbre, physical appearance, clothing, gesture, body odor, and tone of voice, as well as the volume of secretions such as saliva and sweat. But really, even without such things, it's simple enough to get a grasp of his character. He resents his master, he's dissatisfied with this game, and he's on the players' side."

"Weren't you just saying you're *not* an ace detective?"

"I'm saying that when searching for a culprit, I pick them out based on their character. I don't need evidence or alibis—because if I believe they're the culprit, they most certainly are. There is only one condition that needs to be fulfilled for an autocracy to surpass the rule of law, and that is to have a sovereign who never errs. I never misjudge a person. Fal wants to cooperate with the players." Pfle released the wheels of her chair. Her elegant, white palms were dirtied black. She extended her hands to Shadow Gale, who pulled out her handkerchief to wipe them.

"Fal told us the truth," said Pfle, "and the coin is still in circulation. In other words, this has to mean that the one who killed Masked Wonder and stole her items is alive." Once her hands were clean of dirt, the ardor that had filled Pfle's words suddenly cooled. She was back to normal. "Genopsyko Yumenoshima's disappearance is connected to this, too. Someone is up to something."

"So does the lady sovereign who never errs know who that someone is?" Shadow Gale had meant to say that sarcastically, but Pfle's expression was unconcerned as she shrugged.

"I don't know yet. And that's exactly why we should refrain from cooperating with other parties. We can't open our arms and get chummy with someone who might be the enemy, now, can we?"

☆ Detec Bell

Presenting the results of her investigation into Magical Daisy in front of the whole crowd had felt good. Detec Bell had really felt like an ace detective. Even though her life had been in danger then, too, she'd been terribly proud and gotten really into it.

The problems came afterward, once they'd subdued that rioter swinging around the katana.

The leaders' discussion reached no conclusions; it didn't even come close, and then it had ended without going anywhere. They had broken the meeting up early because Nokko wanted to go search for the vanished Genopsyko Yumenoshima. Pfle had said, "Talk to me once you have an objective," and then left, as if this had nothing to do with her. Detec Bell had attempted to win over Clantail, saying that even if it was just the two of them, they should still cooperate, but Clantail's sullen silence had made it hard for Detec Bell to figure out what was on her mind.

Clantail had the lower body of a horse, so when the two faced each other, Clantail ended up looking down on Detec Bell even when they were both sitting down. Plus, the centaur had a tremendous force of presence. Clantail did basically give her a nod at the end, so maybe that meant Detec Bell had gotten her understanding. But since they never decided on anything concrete, that understanding was pointless.

Disappointed and exhausted, Detec Bell returned to the shop in the wasteland town where her party was—and where another draining, disheartening incident awaited.

"She was there! For serious!" Lapis Lazuline was freaking out. Her shoulder-length black hair and kind, pale-brown eyes made her look like a reserved sort of person, but she was always, always noisy.

"Who was here?" asked Detec Bell.

"Genopsyko Yumenoshima," said Melville. She, by contrast, was loud only in looks. Her hairstyle—the quintessence of loud, with curled orange locks dotted with purple flowers—contrasted with the person herself, who was quiet and spoke falteringly. "Genopsyko Yumenoshima, th' lass wha' fell in the waestlan' taun, she 'os watchin' us from 'round yon corner." Melville pointed behind a building.

"No way, I mean, Genopsyko Yumenoshima was—" Detec Bell had been about to say, *"killed in the wasteland town,"* but her lips snapped shut there. Nokko and @Meow-Meow were still searching for her, since it was basically unknown whether she was alive or dead. Detec Bell figured that someone had hidden the body, but since some people still believed that Genopsyko was alive and were looking for her, Detec Bell hesitated to voice her opinion that there was no way a dead person was going to show up.

"She had a real bad stab wound in her face, goin' through her cheek into her mouth and right to the end of her jaw. That was probably where she got cut," said Lazuline, and Melville nodded. "But that wound was stitched up like Frankenstein!" Lazuline cried with a ghoulish expression, and Melville nodded.

"So then what happened?" asked Detec Bell. "Did you call out to her? Did she say anything to you?"

"Well, she wouldn't have been able to talk, anyway. Even her mouth was sewn shut. We were so busy screamin' and freakin' out, I couldn't even begin to try talkin' to her."

It had to have been just Lazuline and Cherna Mouse freaking out. It was difficult to imagine Melville screaming and causing a fuss.

"Anyway, where's Cherna?" Detec Bell asked.

"Genopsyko scampered off somewhere, so Cherna's chasin' her down," Lazuline explained. "Once Cherna brings her back, you'll know we've been tellin' the truth."

"I'm not accusing you of lying."

"Aren't ya? I can almost smell the skepticism rollin' off ya."

They wouldn't lie—but they might have misunderstood what they saw. Lazuline was thoughtless, and Cherna was careless; however, Melville had been with them, too, so that meant Cherna and Lazuline had not just been imagining things. So Genopsyko Yumenoshima really had been there.

The stitches meant either she'd sewn herself up or someone else had. Why would she have done that rather than use recovery medicine? It also didn't make sense that she was going off on her own without letting the others in her party know she was safe. There was no reason for her to do that.

Detec Bell turned her gaze away from Lazuline, who was grabbing her collar and leaning into her, and instead turned to Melville.

The orange-haired girl nodded and, with a jerk of her jaw, indicated just past the shop. "'Ere, she's returned."

A creature leaped out from between two buildings, running on all fours. Right before it was about to collide with Melville, it braked suddenly to a stop. It had left a track on the ground in its wake, and clouds of dust whirled into the air. Ignoring the coughs from Detec Bell and Lapis Lazuline, the figure—Cherna Mouse—lifted her right arm to report, "She wasn't there!"

"Who wasn't there?" asked Detec Bell. "You mean Genopsyko?"

"She just wasn't there—you'd be amazed! Cherna figures she's got to be super-fast. And, and, and what was *really* amazing was that she had no smell at all!"

"Maybe you guys were all just imagining things."

"We weren't! This really happened!" Cherna Mouse shook her

sleeve, and something lightly rolled out of it. There were pockets inside her sleeves, and she typically stored giant sunflower seeds in there.

Melville, Lazuline, and Detec Bell all looked at each other, and then at the thing that had fallen. It was a rock wrapped in a crumpled piece of paper. As the parcel traveled across the ground, the paper unfolded, and they saw inside. Written on the paper in a script that resembled an earthworm wriggling around was a message: *Watch out for the traitor.*

"What's it say?" Cherna asked, unperturbed, but nobody replied.

Melville kicked the rock. Now without its weight, the paper was caught in a gust of wind and flew away.

"Ahh! It's flying away!" Cherna Mouse cried, running after it.

"An' yer meetin'?" Melville asked Detec Bell.

"Oh yeah. We decided we're all going to cooperate."

"Nay, Ah shan't." Melville's eyes never left the rock at their feet. "Some blackguard is schemin', an' we've no inkling who. Cubbe one o' ye in 'is pairty. 'Tis chancy, it is, and we cannae proceed hence."

"But if we all split up at a time like this—"

"Ah'd prefir't to this." Melville said, brooking no argument. Detec Bell couldn't say anything to that.

☆ **Nokko**

Nokko walked around visiting people, but she didn't find Genopsyko. Detec Bell's party claimed to have seen her, so she had to be alive. But Genopsyko never showed herself to Nokko or @Meow-Meow.

Nokko activated the map application, figuring perhaps she could use it in her hunt for Genopsyko, but the location displayed there was the same as @Meow-Meow's. It seemed the map didn't display where the person's position was, but rather her magical phone's. It was entirely useless.

If she's alive, she could at least come see us, Nokko thought—but she never voiced that. @Meow-Meow had hardly said a word since that battle in the town square, and Nokko kept finding her zoning out and staring off into the distance. Nokko tried as hard as she could to transmit fun and happy feelings to her, but she didn't know if it was really working. They had been forced into this life-and-death game, they didn't know where Genopsyko was, and at the end of her battle with that samurai girl, @Meow-Meow had killed her. Even if that girl had been a murderer and a thief, Nokko figured this had to be weighing down on @Meow-Meow along with everything else.

Nokko couldn't say, *"Genopsyko could at least come see us"* or *"I never knew you were that strong, @Meow-Meow!"* or *"Let's all work together to make it out of this alive."* Any of that would dredge up painful memories, and remembering them would just make her even more depressed.

"Not magical girl anymore," @Meow-Meow said suddenly during their meal that day.

Nokko was startled. They were sitting facing each other and ingesting a lifeless meal of preserved rations. @Meow-Meow was silent, and so was Nokko, and their wordless act held no more meaning than reducing their hunger meters. But then @Meow-Meow had suddenly spoken, breaking that silence. Nokko felt like it had been a very long time since she'd last heard the other girl's voice.

"What do you mean, 'not magical girl anymore'?" asked Nokko.

"I mean just what I say. Retired as magical girl."

"Who's retired?"

"Me."

"Huh? You retired from being a magical girl, @Meow-Meow? But you were made to participate in the game anyway?"

"That what happened."

Nokko was about to comfort her, but then she hesitated. It didn't seem like @Meow-Meow had brought this up because of a desire for sympathy, and neither did it seem like just complaining.

It was all words coming from her mouth intermittently. Her face still had this dazed look.

"Something really bad happen. So after, I stop being magical girl."

"Something bad—" Nokko started to say and then stopped. Remembering that would only make @Meow-Meow upset.

"I no remember it at all. It must have been bad enough for me to quit being a magical girl, but I can't remember at all what happened…" With just her front teeth, @Meow-Meow nibbled her nutrition bar, chewing it slowly. "Something awful happened… I quit being a magical girl…but then I participated in this game… like it was totally natural… I didn't think it was strange, either…" She seemed obsessed—possessed, even. Whatever it was, she didn't seem right. She just kept on whispering and muttering. "On top of that building, I was crying. Tears were falling. I was sad. Because I killed someone. Someone I couldn't hold back with. I know that…but…"

She raised her head. There were no clouds in the sky, no stars, no moon. Nothing. There was only sprawling black, and @Meow-Meow's eyes reflected that same darkness. "It was the… the second time? It was the second time, so I thought I could do better…"

There was motion in the thicket, the sound of leaves against leaves. Nokko moved to get up, but @Meow-Meow restrained her with a hand. "Who there?" she asked. There was focus in her eyes and awareness in her voice. The fact that @Meow-Meow was acting normal again was more surprising to Nokko than the fact that someone was there.

"It's me." The magical girl in the wheelchair—and the nurse girl pushing it. Nokko was pretty sure the one in the wheelchair was Pfle. She'd been in a party with Masked Wonder, the murdered girl. The nurse in black was… What was her name again? She was the one who attended Pfle and had leaped in from the side to save her life when she had nearly been killed… Nokko couldn't remember her name.

"I would hope you remember? I'm Pfle, and this is Shadow Gale."

Right. Pfle and Shadow Gale.

"I've come because I have a request," said Pfle. "Would you lend us your ears?"

"I thought we already talk about cooperating with other party," said @Meow-Meow. "If your request help us survive this, we have to listen."

Nokko looked over at @Meow-Meow. There was strength and determination in her eyes. She was thankful that @Meow-Meow had pulled it together, but such a sudden, inexplicable change made Nokko anxious.

"It seems that Detec Bell's team still continues to claim ownership over their territory," said Pfle. "I'm told that those who approach their hunting grounds are threatened by a one-hundred-foot Cherna Mouse."

Magical candy was a necessity for everything here. So of course, you had to gather a lot if you were aiming to complete the game. But stealing from one another would only drive them all farther from completion. The players' solidarity was falling apart. And who would benefit from that? That had to be...

"What they thinking?! This no time to be fighting each other!" Nokko could hear @Meow-Meow's teeth grinding. "We stop them. Having priority on hunting ground don't matter for just finishing game."

"Yes, indeed," Pfle replied. "But I doubt that lot will listen if you try to use words to stop them."

"But I no want us kill each other over it."

"We won't be doing that. I wouldn't want that, either. That's exactly why we need your help."

☆ **Shadow Gale**

The newest unlocked region was now the city area. But despite its title, it was of course not the kind of city you'd see people living in now. It was more of a cyberpunk-style sci-fi area. The aesthetic consisted of jumbled-up cables and wires, and the level design was even more of a mess. It was smaller than the wasteland, the grasslands, and the mountain area had been, but it was like a maze that took some time getting used to.

The shop sold both armor and weapons. They were higher level than the equipment sold at previous shops, too, at +5 power. Shadow Gale bought a +5 weapon and installed it. When she summoned it, she got a wrench and gave it a test swing. It felt incredibly right. These weapons were clearly made with the players in mind. The feeling of the tool rolling in her hand lingered.

The monsters that appeared in this area were robot soldiers that called to mind the androids found in robot anime. According to the encyclopedia, there were four types: attacker, defender, gunner, and general. They attacked with lighting strikes, mini-missiles, body blows, etc., and they were quite a bit stronger than the goblins and skeletons had been.

They were formidable, so they dropped more candy and, what's more, rare items at a rate of about one in a hundred. The shop would buy these arm parts, leg parts, body parts, head parts, etc. at high prices. These items were just vendor trash with no gameplay purpose—for any player other than Shadow Gale, that is.

Shadow Gale's magical ability was modification. Using her wrench and scissors, she could bang away at things to improve them. She'd always used her magic for tasks that were simple but nonetheless made people happy, like improving TV picture quality, upping the gas mileage of a car, or increasing disk storage on a computer.

Right now, Shadow Gale's hands were whipping about, using parts of every type to modify Pfle's wheelchair. They'd requested the other parties gather the materials. When they had declared they would duel with Cherna Mouse, the others had all gladly cooperated. Shadow Gale understood quite well just how much everyone hated that party. Pfle had also asked @Meow-Meow to deliver the things they needed as well as help gather them. All this intensive modification had made the wheelchair dramatically less mobile and decreased how long it would work, so it helped a lot to be moving around less.

They accumulated more and more parts. No matter how Shadow Gale used them up, they never disappeared. She could see no end to the grind.

Pfle was using her magical phone. She seemed to be reading something.

"Um…," Shadow Gale began.

"What is it, Mamori?"

"How long should I keep doing this…?"

"Until it's satisfactory," Pfle answered.

Who was Shadow Gale supposed to satisfy, and how? She got the feeling that asking those questions wouldn't get her any answers. "Could I ask one thing…?"

"What is it?"

"While working on this, I've been thinking about a lot of things."

"That's some pretty impressive multitasking, for you."

"I've been thinking about who killed Masked Wonder."

"Oh?"

"I think it could be @Meow-Meow." Shadow Gale thought that was a pretty outrageous thing to have said. But contrary to her expectations, Pfle just kept fiddling with her phone with no apparent concern. Shadow Gale sullenly went back to her task. She continued on with that for a few more minutes, until Pfle broke the silence.

"Mamori…when you suspect someone, you feel a need to have some sort of basis for your suspicions, don't you? You're a different sort from me."

Most human beings were a different sort from Pfle. It took talent to become that arrogant. "Yes, more or less," Shadow Gale replied.

"Tell me your reasoning for why you believe @Meow-Meow to be the culprit. I'll listen."

"When she fought the samurai in the square, she attacked by summoning boulders."

"Oh, yes. Seems like quite the convenient magic to have," Pfle remarked.

@Meow-Meow had pulled rocks and buildings from those slips of paper, and then afterward, she'd sucked that building she'd summoned right back into the paper, too. Both of the things she used to fight had been everywhere in this game so far. It seemed @Meow-Meow's power was to seal things inside her talismans.

Shadow Gale continued, "And Masked Wonder's head was crushed by a boulder, right?"

"…That's your basis? Because @Meow-Meow was using boulders? That's all?"

"Of course that's not all. It's ultimately just one of many elements that make her suspicious."

"Oh? So then what's the main reason you suspect her?"

"The coin." Shadow Gale spun the wrench and cut with the shears. Her power of modification wasn't based on any reason or principle, so she didn't really understand the point of each of her individual actions as she worked. "@Meow-Meow put that massive slice of building inside her talisman," Shadow Gale explained. "If she can pull off something that extreme, then she might have an even higher-level technique for storing data itself inside her talismans without going through the magical phone. She may be capable of carrying the coin around with her without installing it." Magical girls' powers ignored rules and principles. It was just like how Shadow Gale could use the robot soldiers' rare drops for a purpose other than sale. "If the culprit is someone else, I don't know how they would be carrying the coin around without a magical phone. So, to summarize, that's why I think she might be the culprit." Shadow Gale finished off her explanation like an elementary school child would close an essay.

When she glanced toward Pfle, the other girl's eyes had not left her phone. "Your deductions aren't bad."

"Right?"

"Perhaps I've misjudged you."

Exactly what kind of person had Kanoe thought her to be?

☆ Detec Bell

Becoming a magical girl offered many opportunities to observe many strange things, starting with the girl herself. But still, not many of them would see something as unreal as this.

It had to be a mile or two away, but even so, the feeling that the brutal conflict might spill all the way over to them kept Detec Bell on edge. Even their slightest motions created intense dust clouds and noise. The one-hundred-foot Cherna Mouse and the one-hundred-foot... What would you call it? At a glance, it resembled a crab. Of course, it wasn't really a crustacean. It was entirely mechanical. Pfle had called it a ten-legged tank, hadn't she?

The ground rumbled and dust billowed up as Cherna Mouse ran to make a grab at the tank, which it blocked. Detec Bell could sense the sound and impact of their struggle all the way where she was.

Two of the machine's legs grappled with Cherna's arms, while one of the other eight legs took the opportunity to strike her side, causing her to lose her balance and fall over. Clouds of dust obscured her from Detec Bell's vision, but still, Cherna Mouse rolled away from the tank, knocking over the high-rises in her way, cracking them underneath her massive frame, crushing them to the point where it hurt just to look at them.

Cherna Mouse withdrew, but the tank didn't give chase. It stood firm. Then a protrusion where a crab's eyes would be flashed, and something exploded a ways ahead of the tank. The tank had fired its lasers. It launched Cherna Mouse back and sent her rolling along the ground. Three buildings were destroyed in the exchange, but they were behind the tank now, and Detec Bell couldn't see them from where she stood.

Even from atop a distant high-rise, Detec Bell could grasp the massive scale of this destruction. Melville was squinting her right eye a bit. Every time Cherna Mouse was attacked, Lapis Lazuline yipped, which was highly annoying.

Detec Bell could see where this battle was headed. The ten-legged tank was overwhelming Cherna. It had more methods of attack available to it, it moved fast, and it was also equipped with projectile weapons. Detec Bell never would have imagined that any magical girl could beat Cherna Mouse, but at this rate, she would go down.

It seemed like Melville and Lazuline didn't want her to lose, but Detec Bell wouldn't really mind. Maybe it would be better if she did.

That morning, they'd received a request.

"I would like to propose a nonlethal duel."

The visitors came to Detec Bell's party while they were eating breakfast. It was the magical girl in the wheelchair and the nurse in the black outfit...the Pfle and Shadow Gale pair. The very first thing out of Pfle's mouth was an invitation to duel, creating a lot of question marks in their heads. But what Pfle said next clarified her intentions.

"If we win, we want you to stop monopolizing hunting grounds. You use the threat of force to back your actions. If we demonstrate our superior strength, then you wouldn't mind stepping down, I take it? I believe Miss Melville over there has said that the strong rule."

Promising they would give their answer later, Detec Bell had Pfle and Shadow Gale leave. She had the sense not to quarrel in front of another party.

"Is it true that you're blocking the others from our hunting grounds?" Detec Bell asked Cherna Mouse.

"Yep." Cherna Mouse didn't seem in the least bit shy about it.

"Why would you do something like that? I thought we said that we all have to cooperate."

"Cherna doesn't care about that stuff," she replied.

In order to unlock the gate to the next area, they had to get into the office in front of the city area's defense headquarters, and for that, they needed a password. Detec Bell had tried to discuss this with the other parties, but their response hadn't been positive. They'd hardly managed to have a conversation. Now Detec Bell knew why.

"Don't give me that," she said. "It's not too late. Go and apologize. You can bring a gift for them, too, if you like."

"No. Cherna hasn't done anything wrong. If we're gonna have a duel, Cherna'll beat 'em up."

This wasn't going anywhere. She was not the kind of person who could be compelled to obey.

"Fightin's never good, y'know?" Lazuline said, nodding with folded arms and a smug expression. She would be no help.

Detec Bell turned to Melville. "Make her stop."

"Ah shan't." Melville's gaze flicked downward. Her eyelashes stirred in the wind.

That was it. Cherna Mouse wouldn't just go off on her own and do whatever she wanted. She always listened to what Melville said.

"Did Ah no' tell ye? 'Ere be a vill'n among's. To discuss't'd be fer naught. Ye cannae unnerstan'."

"Melvy's sayin' we can't cooperate with people, since one of them might be a bad guy," Lazuline translated.

"But if you're going to be like that, then—" If Melville was going to bring that up, then there was also no guarantee that the bad guy wasn't one of their own party... But that remark caught in Detec Bell's throat. She just couldn't say it. She bit her lip and tasted a little blood.

Cherna Mouse's magic was simple: She could make herself bigger. It was simple but powerful. If a large enemy hit you, it hurt, but hitting a large enemy in return wasn't really effective. Cherna had demonstrated her immense strength to them in their battles with monsters. Frankly, all they really needed in their party was this one giant monster—er, Cherna Mouse.

What's more, their opponent had picked the wasteland as the duel's location. It was a wide-open area, the kind of space where

Cherna Mouse was at her greatest advantage. It was a sprawling plain with only high-rises dotted here and there. Those wouldn't get in the way.

Cherna had ignored Detec Bell's attempt to hold her back and had accepted the duel. One hour later, the hamster girl was already enormous, ready and waiting for her opponent. Detec Bell, Melville, and Lazuline observed from the roof of a distant building.

With the wasteland as their battleground, who would even be able to oppose this monster? Detec Bell was wondering, when @Meow-Meow trudged her way to the duel site. *Is she going to be the one fighting? She's strong, for sure, but it'd be a pretty tough fight for her.*

But that wasn't what was going on. @Meow-Meow tossed out a talisman and ran away. The slip of paper fluttered downward to explode with a *boof!* When the smoke cleared, a massive mechanical crab was standing there.

Its abdominal section was round. The glowing parts where a crab's eyes would have been had to be sensors or something. From what Detec Bell could see of the layer edges, a number of armored plates had been sheeted over one another. The thickness of that armor made the tank seem like it would be slow, but the ten legs extending from its torso maneuvered with quick little movements. Each leg had two joints and a sharp point at the end. The limbs were covered in thick, metallic, armor-like plates on the front side, whirring, rattling, and clicking mechanically with every movement. The whole thing shone a metallic black, and the tank had no square parts. It was rounded in every way. Unlike a real crab, it had nothing resembling pincers, so it resembled a spider, aside from its number of legs. It was about the same size as Cherna Mouse and perhaps heavier. Basically, it was huge.

With Pfle on her back, Shadow Gale ran up one of the crab's legs, opened up the lid on its torso, and literally kicked her in before she closed the lid and scrambled back down.

"Shall we begin the duel, then?" The voice was loud, probably amplified by speakers, but it was definitely Pfle's.

Cherna Mouse was surprised, but she didn't back away. She approached to grapple with the machine, and the duel began.

Cherna Mouse was at a disadvantage. It was looking bad for her—she'd never be able to win at this rate. And to be honest, Detec Bell wanted her to lose. She'd made them into real hypocrites by being so uncooperative with other parties. If Cherna lost this, that would satisfy everyone else, and it would probably make working with them easier.

Cherna Mouse's whole body was trembling like she was ill as she crouched down, crossing her arms over her eyes. She appeared to be protecting herself from attacks. Seeing her misery under the barrage of blows hurt to watch.

"We should make her stop. Cherna's already lost," Detec Bell said, looking over toward Melville, who was facing the battleground with a calm expression. "At this rate, worst-case scenario—Cherna gets killed. They said this would be bloodless, but sometimes people get impulses."

"Shield yer ears," was all Melville replied.

Cherna braced her legs wide on the ground, crouching down. Knees bent, arms spread wide, she opened her mouth so big it covered a third of her face, and her throat vibrated in a howl. The heavy-looking tank reeled, staggered, bowed backward, and then dug its claws into the ground to withstand the roar. Nearby buildings crumbled and collapsed. Clouds of dust blew away.

An instant before, Detec Bell had plugged her ears, opened her mouth, and thrown herself to the ground. The booming noise made everything shiver and shake as Cherna screamed and raged. This had never happened before. The giant magical girl extended her arms in front of her, leaning forward as she turned to face the ten-legged tank.

Detec Bell rubbed her eyes. Something was odd. She'd thought Cherna Mouse was stationary, but it looked like she was approaching them.

The crab's eyes flashed, and another beam hit its mark. But this explosion was far smaller than the previous ones had been. Cherna

Mouse's hamster suit was already black with soot, and the explosion was so small, it only added one more black soot spot on her. She didn't even wobble.

Then Detec Bell realized—Cherna Mouse wasn't getting closer. The explosions weren't shrinking. Cherna Mouse was *growing*. She was already twice…two and a half times…three times larger than the crab, and she was still expanding.

A black sphere about two yards in diameter fired from the hull of the crab into the distance before it landed and rolled away. But before Detec Bell had the time to wonder what it was, Cherna Mouse had taken half a step forward, closing the distance between her and the crab, and stomped it flat.

Detec Bell looked up at the sky.

☆ Pechka

They'd been deceived. If they died in the game, they would die in real life, too. But they couldn't escape now. They had to keep playing the game. There was no other choice.

Next after the city area came the subterranean level. After passing through the gates, they emerged in a little room, removed the lid on the floor there, and descended through it to find an underground world. It wasn't like a man-made dungeon, but more a natural cave, like a limestone hollow. It was all damp and slippery, floor included. Pechka raised her right foot up too high and fell, and when Nonako tried to catch her, they both went down together. Pechka hit her waist hard and felt ready to cry.

It was a cave, but not small at all. In fact, it was huge, about four times Pechka's height to the ceiling. The width of the path varied a lot depending on location as it progressed, but it was generally pretty big.

Still, because it was a cave, it was chilly and damp and not at all a comfortable place to be.

Pfle and Cherna Mouse's giant monster one-on-one had ended in Cherna Mouse's victory. Pfle's escape pod had saved her life. If not for that, she certainly would have died. Pechka had been so frightened, she'd stopped watching halfway through, so she had learned the whole story from Nonako Miyokata's and Rionetta's recaps.

Pechka thought that Pfle had done well. No other magical girl would have been able to stand against Cherna Mouse—she would have chased them off, and that would have been the end of it. They had gone to a lot of trouble to gather up all those parts, but still, none of them blamed Pfle for her loss. They expressed their appreciation with "You did well" or "You did your best," and then they left. Pfle had failed to stop Detec Bell's party, but Pechka figured that at least counted as firing a strike back.

The next day, the subterranean area was unlocked. They said that Pfle had been the one to decipher the cryptography quest in the city area that would unlock the next region. Pfle had simultaneously been preparing for the match against Cherna Mouse and finishing off that unlock quest. No one was offering gratitude now.

The scouters, Pechka and Nonako, ended up working together with the combat team, though not because the exploration team was useless. They hadn't completed any of the area unlock quests, but they had done some side quests to earn items and candy. No, it was simply because the game had become too difficult to be splitting up their forces. The enemies in the subterranean area were strong. The Rionetta and Clantail team aside, it was a real struggle for Nonako to fight while managing a burden—Pechka. The weapons they'd bought in the city area were sturdy and easy to wield, but that didn't mean they could somehow muddle through on strength of weapons alone.

Rionetta had really been the one to push for this plan. Reasonably, they would need the cooperation of every player to beat this game. But some of the players were refusing to work together. In that case, they should at least work on their own party's sense of unity. Rionetta spoke passionately, and she had Clantail nodding. Then Rionetta had scooted over to Pechka and whispered in her ear. "You needn't worry. I'll keep you safe, Pechka."

Nonako Miyokata decided to complain about this. "What are you getting all cozy with her for?"

"It's none of your business."

"Pechka and I were on the exploration team together! We are *les sœurs* now! Basically sisters!"

"And which fine nation does *that* logic originate from?"

As usual, they were at each other's throats. Knowing they could die put everyone on edge, and they were frustrated because they didn't want to play this stupid game that they were forced to participate in.

Still, things seemed to have improved, and that might have been because now, they had accepted Pechka. Thrice daily, during their mealtimes, she was the star of the show. Even outside of mealtimes, they continued to respect her, due to her mealtime celebrity. With each spoonful, Rionetta would put a hand to her cheek, and Nonako Miyokata would praise her to bits with random French thrown in. Their joy in her creations was what made Pechka eager to cook.

Walking down the underground passage, very occasionally, they would emerge in dome-shaped open areas. There, dragons would appear. But though they were called "dragons," they were only about two yards long, with a wingspan of four, and were a lot smaller than what one might generally imagine dragons to be, if asked to do so for a fantasy story. But even so, they weren't easy enemies to fight.

A translucent thread shot from Clantail's rear, tangling up a dragon's wing. The creature screeched an uncanny, birdlike screech and tried to fly away, dragging her along as it flailed about. Using all eight of her spider legs, Clantail clung to a boulder, bracing herself and refusing to let go. The two strained against each other, and then Rionetta calculated just the right moment to jump in, when both of them were locked in place, and reached out far with her right arm to swipe the dragon with her claws. She ripped open the dragon's neck, hard scales and all. Its blue armor fluttered to the ground, and then red blood followed, gushing like the water of a dramatic fountain.

Ever since they'd begun fighting in the subterranean area, Clantail had spent more time with her lower body transformed into a massive spider. Her poisonous-looking yellow-and-black pattern, the rustling noises her legs made as they moved, and the massive size of her abdomen were so frightening, they made every hair on Pechka's body stand on end. Just getting near Clantail made her feel faint. *I wish she'd do her usual cute deer or pony*, she thought, but it seemed that a spider had better grip underground. A hoofed animal would slip more easily.

The dragon fell from the sky, the impact of its face-first plunge sending a tremor through the earth. Now that Rionetta and Clantail had finished their dragon, they changed their equipment and faced the one Nonako Miyokata had been fending off. This time, all three of them ganged up on it. There was one more dragon engaged in an aerial battle with another of its kind, but when all three magical girls turned to face it, they overwhelmed their enemy and took it down before long.

Aside from Pechka, who hadn't been participating in the battle, they were all wounded in some way. They made use of the recovery items stored with Pechka to heal their injuries. The one most heavily hurt was Nonako's familiar, the dragon.

That goblin Nonako had cooed over so much had been relieved of its post the moment they had defeated a dragon. Now the dragon was the one decorated with a ribbon. When she had dismissed the goblin, it had tried to flee, but the dragon had killed it with a strike from behind. Upon witnessing that, Nonako had cried, "*Oh là là! Strong! Powerful! Cute!*" She was elated. Apparently, she was not at all attached to the goblin she'd been coddling not so long before. Was this what they called "continental rationalism"? Pechka really had no idea.

They walked in search of dragons, and whenever they found a place that seemed good, Cherna Mouse would drive them away. So they'd go somewhere else to find dragons, beat them, gather up the candy and rare drops, and then use that candy to buy recovery items and other things. The shop in the subterranean town sold protection charms, such as the red charm that would guard against fire elemental enemies. Some fine technique was required to employ the different charms depending on the type of dragon.

The party had given up on exploration. If they were all going to be in one group, then it was more effective to focus on grinding rather than searching around. Their approach was to just leave it to the others, since some other party would just unlock areas anyway. Nobody said that out loud, but they had to be thinking it. At least, Pechka was. They left game progression to the others, and since the good hunting grounds were occupied, they didn't really feel like they should be cooperating. So they just ground for candy with the pessimistic rationale of *"Well, this is better than doing nothing."*

And if anyone was going to be categorized as "doing nothing," it was Pechka. She was only ever useful as a mule for their items. But no one complained. Far from it—she was cordially welcomed. The entire party looked forward to eating, and when mealtime was near, her food gave them all a boost of energy. They'd acquired some utensils from *R*, so now she could make a greater variety of dishes. The others were overjoyed, telling her how delicious and wonderful it all was.

It's fine this way, thought Pechka. *If things go on like this and nothing more happens, it'll be fine. It'll be…*

That was when their magical phones rang, informing them that it was time for their pre-logout forced transport.

☆ **Nokko**

Three days had passed, and the magical girls had gathered once again in the wasteland town. The atmosphere in the square was dour. Cherna Mouse had beaten Pfle, and Detec Bell's party was celebrating the height of their fortunes…or not, apparently. Detec Bell was by herself, a significant distance away from the other two. Maybe things weren't going well among them.

Pfle had lost her wheelchair. Nokko had heard that the ten-legged tank had just been her wheelchair with modifications.

And the tank had been smashed up—so in other words, her wheel-chair was gone. But she seemed cheerful regardless. Shadow Gale carried her piggyback as the two of them discussed something. Pfle had also been the one to unlock the subterranean area. That she had the shrewdness required to both unlock an area and pre-pare that weapon concurrently made Nokko vaguely fearful.

As for Clantail's party…Nonako Miyokata and Rionetta were squabbling. Nokko couldn't hear what it was about, but just seeing them inches from grabbing each other, Nokko could easily imag-ine the kind of foul language they had to be abusing each other with. Clantail and Pechka weren't even watching, acting as if noth-ing was happening at all.

It seemed @Meow-Meow had cheered up a little since all that had happened. Genopsyko still hadn't shown up, but just the fact that she was apparently still alive was reason enough to be grateful. The information from Detec Bell's party about how they had wit-nessed Genopsyko Yumenoshima was ambiguous and uncertain, but it was something to cling to. "I'm sure Yumenoshima have her reasons," @Meow-Meow had said, and she seemed to have more energy now. She wasn't lost in her anguish like before.

The monsters in the subterranean area were strong. Nokko had an attack elemental modification charm and was equipped with a Mop +5, but even then, it was a real struggle. Still, @Meow-Meow crushed the monsters with her summons and her martial arts, and somehow they had made it through to this point with a party of two.

Then Nokko had an idea. Two and two. If they could meet up with Pfle and Shadow Gale and form a single party… Once her train of thought reached that point, she remembered Genopsyko and promptly dropped that idea. Genopsyko was alive. Even if she wasn't with them now, they couldn't act like she'd never been there. Remove her from their party? Never. @Meow-Meow had been so stubborn about her. She would never agree.

In the fountain that occupied the center of the square, someone's magical phone lay faceup. This was a familiar sight now—though Nokko didn't want it to be. After a little waiting, the phone turned on and a hologram appeared, floating in the air. "I'd like to thank you all very much for gathering here, pon."

The last time, they'd welcomed Fal with harsh jeers. But he was just as he was before, merely floating there, seemingly emotionless, as if all of that had been a dream. None of them would bother to rail anymore. It wasn't constructive. It would be difficult to call it proactive. And it wouldn't solve anything. But most of all, Nokko just felt like they'd all become apathetic.

"Today is group logout day, pon. At sunset, you will all log out together. As with last time, we plan to have you log in again after three days in the real world have passed for maintenance purposes, pon." Fal twirled on a horizontal axis, scattering gold scales. "Just like before, there will now be a random special event. This time, the event is…" Fal's voice cut off. They were all waiting for it to continue, but it was silent, frozen. Pfle had beaten them all by a wide margin during the previous event. What would this one be?

The image of Fal shrank and then stretched. Noise ran across it, distorting the picture. Fal was expressionless but, mysteriously, still appeared abnormal. "…Everyone, please check the amount of magical candy on your phones, pon."

Nokko checked her phone. Total candy: 2,651. Being a party of two, they didn't have to split the candy up as many ways. But they were surely less effective at monster extermination than a party of four would be. She and @Meow-Meow had only purchased a minimal amount of items: recovery medicine, the monster encyclopedia, attack elemental modification charms, travel passes, weapons for each of them, and a teleporter. But still, their candy stores had to be low compared to those of the other parties.

"Fifteen minutes from now," said Fal, "the player who holds the smallest amount of candy will die, pon."

The square went dead silent. After a few seconds, the square was filled with hissing and fierce roars of anger.

Once again, Nonako Miyokata and Rionetta were quarreling. "This is *exactly* why I told you not to squander all that candy on *R*!" accused Rionetta.

"*Mon dieu*, and who was it scarfing down all that food? You were like, 'It's so good, it's so good!'"

The other members of their party made no move to stop them, and the other groups were too busy raging at Fal to even consider intervening.

The little spheroid just repeated the same message. "It can't be changed now, pon. Your understanding, please, pon. I will repeat it one more time, pon. Fifteen minutes from now, the player who holds the smallest amount of candy will die, pon. The player who holds the smallest amount of candy will die, pon."

Nokko was thinking. You could transfer candy to someone else. And likewise, you could receive it, too. In other words, you could steal it. This whole "fifteen minutes" thing—that was just giving the stronger girls some extra time to steal candy from the weak, wasn't it? She glanced around. They were all in discussions with only their own party members, more or less, including the ones who were yelling at one another. So then if it did turn into a scramble, they'd probably steal from other parties. That left Nokko and @Meow-Meow's smaller team in a bad position.

Nokko was horrified—then she panicked and erased that feeling. She didn't squeeze her eyes shut and optimistically reassure herself that that sort of thing would never happen. What she did was make sure that her feelings of horror wouldn't be transmitted around.

Many of them had to have realized the unspoken reality here: This was an endorsement for them to steal from one another. Nokko considered that perhaps she should do something before anyone else figured it out. Pfle and Shadow Gale were a party of two as well, and Pfle was weaponless to boot, being carried around by Shadow Gale. But when Nokko looked over to that party, she saw Pfle was facing Fal.

"Fal." Even among the chaotic squabbling, her voice carried. Nokko, far away as she was, could hear her question to the mascot. "You said the player who holds the smallest sum of candy. So what happens if it's not a player, but *players*? Will one be chosen at random? Or will multiple people die at once?"

Fal paused a moment. "In the case that there is more than one person who has the smallest amount of candy, then no one will be chosen, pon. The event would end with zero deaths, pon."

Hearing that, Pfle wore a nasty smile. "Are you relieved to have someone notice that 'player, singular' part?"

Fal ignored Pfle and repeated the announcement. "I repeat, pon. In the case that there is more than one person with the smallest amount of candy, no one will be chosen, pon. The event will end with zero deaths, pon."

There was something of a commotion.

"In other word," said @Meow-Meow, "we should just temporary make everyone's candy same number, right?"

"What? Cherna doesn't wanna give up candy," Cherna Mouse protested.

Detec Bell countered, "We just have to return everyone's original amount once the event is over. That'd be allowed, right?"

"Of course, pon. Once the event is over, the amount of candy in your possession will no longer have any meaning, pon."

"Maybe it'd be easiest to understand if we just made everyone's candy zero," said Lapis Lazuline.

Rionetta scoffed. "So we would buy items to zero our balance? Or discard all our magical candy? I decline either."

"How about gathering it all on one person's phone *magique*?" suggested Nonako Miyokata.

"What if she absconds wi' the whole lot? I'll be trustin' no lass here with our candy."

Lazuline interpreted for everyone. "Melvy is sayin', we'd all be in trouble if they just took everythin', right? Right now, there's no one here we can trust with everybody's candy. So...how 'bout takin' it all out of our phones?"

"Um, magical candy is ultimately just a number, pon. You can't take it out, so please be careful, pon."

"Well then, how about we calculate the average of the group and set all our candy at that number?" suggested Rionetta.

"Let's go with that," said Pfle. "Everyone, report the number of candy you hold. Don't over- or underreport it. Be honest and inform us as to the amount you have. And don't forget to check your neighbors' phones, too."

When Pfle added "And don't forget to check your neighbors' phones, too" like an afterthought, Nokko sensed that some hidden malice was surfacing. But still, she was relieved that they wouldn't have to steal from one another.

The curses, wails, and cries of anger disappeared, and they all quietly set into action. Nokko didn't even have to influence their emotions. Magical girls were realistic and practical, and that still held true when they were using fantastical magic and being forced to play a kill-or-be-killed game. Wherever, whenever, whoever the magical girl, if shown a good way to go about things, she would cooperate and take that option.

They all reported the amounts of candy they held, and Pfle calculated the average in her head. There was a remainder of three, but it was decided that Pfle would take the extras. It would work just fine as long as there were multiple people holding the smallest amount in the end.

What was surprising was that @Meow-Meow and Nokko's candy reserves were actually higher than average. They hadn't been proactively grinding like the other parties competing for hunting grounds, and the only other thing you could spend candy on was R. Was there some quest or other that required candy?

@Meow-Meow pulled out Genopsyko's phone, too. The amount of candy on it hadn't changed. It had been at the same number since they finished that unlock quest, so now that the monsters were dropping more candy, her stores were comparatively low. Nokko helped manage Genopsyko's phone, adding and subtracting candy from the other magical girls.

The only sounds in the square were the beeps of their magical phones. They all surrounded the fountain in a circle as they exchanged candy, monitoring one another for any strange behavior. Before long, the numbers on their phones had evened out, and all of them, aside from Pfle, ended up with the lowest number.

Three more minutes to go until the time limit Fal had announced. Pfle, carried by Shadow Gale, walked to each girl and her magical phone, checking to see that there were no errors.

She gave the thumbs-up. "It's okay!"

The beeping of the phones stopped, and some of the girls began chatting with the others nearby. Pfle told them all to "Keep your eyes on the phones of your neighbors!" But even so, the atmosphere had relaxed. Nokko looked at @Meow-Meow beside her. Their eyes met.

"Is relief, huh?" said @Meow-Meow.

"…Yeah. It is," Nokko replied.

All of their phones rang. The time had come. Fal announced, "Holding the smallest amount of candy is…huh?"

A magical phone bounced on the ground with a clatter, and its owner followed, landing on her back. For some reason, she fell slowly, sleeves fluttering, hair flowing. The moment she collapsed, her sunflower seeds scattered around her. The device hit the girl's body and fell over, coming to a stop by her head. The light from it illuminated the girl's profile. Her expression was vacant, not understanding what had happened.

"The one holding the smallest amount…was…Cherna Mouse… pon."

MASTER SIDE #4

"I can't take this anymore, pon. People are dying, pon. I can't let you keep doing this, pon." The strain in Fal's voice escalated further.

"Why not? Things are just getting started now, right?" The girl seemed more relaxed. Her right hand left her glasses so she could snap her fingers, and the noise changed the images in the monitors.

Magical girls appeared on every one of the screens covering the floor, walls, and ceiling. The fallen Cherna Mouse. Akane, crushed by the building. Masked Wonder, her head smashed in, then a rock dropped on her once she was down. Magical Daisy and her blown-out torso. The rows of monitors, large and small, displayed the brutal images of the magical girls' bodies.

With its beady little red-and-black eyes, Fal glared at each of the monitors in turn and then lowered its gaze. Its holographic body blurred, noise running through it. "Fal's ha...enough...don't kill an...ore people..." It wasn't just its image that was warping. Its voice was distorted with grating static, too, as its pitch randomly shifted between high and low.

The girl smiled. "How *awful* of you to say that. When exactly did I kill anyone? What happened with Magical Daisy was an unfortunate accident. After that, they started killing one another on their own. I only set the stage. Whether they get along or go for one another's throats is up to them."

The noise in Fal's hologram cleared, and its eyes lifted toward the girl. "That's just your excuse! Master is the one who incited them to start killing one another, and master is the one who created the arena, pon!"

"But, like, that's just how this sort of test works. The *proper* way for magical girls to act in this situation would be to band together and attempt to escape, not to hurt each other. Riiight?"

"But even Magical Daisy at the start— You clearly meant harm by placing an enemy that reflects projectiles so early in the game, pon! That wasn't an accident, pon!"

"You're being paranoid. Magical Daisy just wasn't as cautious as she should've been."

Like a ball hitting the floor, Fal's body squashed flat, stretched, and shrank, its synthetic voice producing sounds resembling anguish. The girl took no notice of Fal's pain, smirking.

"...I sent a message to the Magical Kingdom a little while ago," said Fal. "I reported everything: what's being done here right now and who's been making these girls kill one another, pon."

"Oh, really?" the girl replied, still smirking.

CHAPTER 5

THE BIG DRAGON AND
THE CHINESE GIRL

☆ **Pechka**

Cherna Mouse fell. What happened after that, Pechka watched with total detachment.

Someone checked Cherna Mouse's magical phone, yelling out that it was one candy short. Another blamed Pfle for this, since she'd been the one checking all the phones, yet another took her side, defending her, and then they were all squabbling. Everyone seemed uneasy. They had gone with a method Fal had assured them would work out, and for some reason, it had failed. They discussed and shouted and foisted the blame on one another, contending, debating what happened with this, what was going on with that, and still they reached no conclusion. When they tried to ask Fal, he seemed confused as to what had happened. They were getting nowhere.

Detec Bell's party left the square to go bury Cherna Mouse,

and the other groups split off. Vague anxieties remained in Pechka's heart. She was hit with the realization that sometimes, people would die, and they wouldn't understand why.

Just being dragged into this game and forced to play at the risk of her own life was enough to make her head spin, but the ambiguous rules ensured they had no idea how they might die, or for what reasons.

It had been about two hours since Cherna Mouse's death. Rionetta and Nonako Miyokata continued to bicker right up until their return to the real world. Clantail was clopping her hooves in irritation, while Pechka gazed up at the sky. It was pitch-black: no stars, moons, or clouds.

When Rionetta and Nonako noticed that Pechka was looking up at the empty sky, they stopped bickering and lifted their eyes, too. Clantail stopped tapping her hooves and followed suit.

Rionetta muttered, "Hunting will be easier now."

Cherna Mouse had been the gatekeeper helping her party squat on the good hunting spots. With her gone, no one would complain if Pechka's party wanted to go to those places. In fact, their party was now the only one to still have all four members. *So then doesn't that mean we're the strongest in a fight right now?* Pechka wondered, and then she was sorry for even having thought of that. When she looked at the others—not counting Rionetta, who'd been the one to say it out loud—Nonako was nodding, and it seemed she and Clantail were thinking the same thing. That just distressed Pechka even more.

The first thing that Chika did when she was back in reality was turn her attention to the sky. Clouds obscured two-thirds of the waxing crescent moon, and dark gray masses blocked the stars, too. Even so, it looked like a proper night sky. She was grateful to have come back to see it.

When Chika got up the next morning, she washed her face, put some incense on the family altar before breakfast, and pressed her hands together. This had never been a custom of hers, and she wasn't terribly devout, but she had nothing else to cling to. Her little brother laughed at her, her parents seemed concerned, and her grandfather praised her for it with a comment that he was impressed. But Chika wasn't really paying attention to her family's reactions. She focused earnestly on her prayer. She was aware that it looked silly, but still, she would cling to anything that might give her hope.

She zoned out a lot at school, and she had nearly run into a telephone pole en route. In class, the teacher pointed out her inattention, earning sniggers from the class. Chika, who had always tried to avoid standing out, was now the butt of ridicule. In the past, that might have made her mope for a week, but now it didn't really bother her.

If she let her mind wander, her thoughts would always return to the game. Her motivations were not completion oriented, like *How can we unlock the next area?* or *The monsters in that spot are great for grinding.* Half of them were wishes for everything to be okay, and the other half were sick imaginings of her premature death.

During her book club time, she left her seat for half an hour. When her friends showed concern, she put up a tough front, smiling and telling them she was fine. Then she rushed back home, transformed into Pechka, dug up some dirt from the garden, and threw it into a pot to make a boxed lunch: rolled omelets, bacon-wrapped asparagus, wieners cut to look like octopuses, rice with seaweed sprinkles, fried chicken, mini tomatoes, and a cooked spinach *ohitashi* salad. She packed some fruit in a separate plastic container.

Examining the contents of this lunch box, she thought it looked a little childish. She'd made it according to her own preferences, thinking it might be fun to eat such a lunch, and this was the result. *Maybe I should do some research on a cooking website,* she thought.

She then got changed and headed to the baseball grounds. On the way, she helped an old man who was loading his mini-truck with daikon radishes. He thanked her, and she replied with a smile, while internally, she was scoffing at herself for assisting people at a time like this. This was just another method of escaping reality.

Ninomiya literally came running to her. The baseball grounds had the facilities for night games, so to keep the darkness at bay, they put on glittering lights as they practiced. In the summertime, bugs gathered around the bright bulbs, including rhinoceros beetles and stag beetles, and that attracted kids and hobbyists with no interest in baseball.

Ninomiya wolfed down the lunch as fast as he could so that he would be on time for his evening practice, and when he was done, he faced Pechka with his hands together and bowed in appreciation. "Thank you so much for the food." She was happy to receive his gratitude, but it was a little embarrassing.

While Ninomiya ate, Pechka just sat together with him on the bench, placing about two empty seats' worth of space between them, and watched. If their eyes happened to meet by accident, he might realize that she had been staring at him the whole time, so she occasionally looked away, observing him in glances as he enjoyed the meal.

He had scrapes from shaving—and occasional bits of facial hair he'd missed. They were in the same class, and Chika thought of herself as still a child, but Ninomiya was already doing the same things as an adult man. His cheeks and jaw moved in time with the rising and falling of his sturdy chest. Acne faintly marked his cheeks—that part of him was still boyish. He'd run all this way after practice, so he was sweating. This close to him, the scent of his sweat reached her nose, making her blush even deeper. He was scarfing the food down but holding his chopsticks in the proper manner. He seemed like the son of a good family, and she liked that.

There was some rice stuck to his cheek. *Should I point it out?* she wondered. *Would it be okay for me to pluck it off him? It would definitely be a bad idea to take it and put it in my own mouth. So if I wrap it in a tissue and throw it away, that wouldn't come off as gross, would it?* But while she was busy worrying about it, Ninomiya wiped the offending grain off his cheek with a finger and popped it in his mouth.

This was all she did on the first day—observed his face and eating habits. She didn't talk much. Just thinking about saying something to him made her nervous, and she didn't want to bother him. He was focused on stuffing his cheeks and enjoying the food.

But on the second day, Ninomiya started talking to her. Chika was already aware that he was more of a chatterbox than might be expected. He talked enthusiastically about all sorts of things: how he'd been batting well lately; how the coach would sometimes bring his dog, which was big and scary-looking; how when he'd tried practicing a knuckle ball, the coach had gotten angry at him and told him to stop fooling around; and how the bicycle he rode to school was broken, so now he was running to school. Lots of things. Pechka was happy to watch Ninomiya enjoying himself.

But then he asked, "What about you?" And Pechka didn't know how to answer.

She realized that Pechka couldn't talk about herself. She couldn't say, *"I'm a magical girl,"* and neither could she say, *"I'm being forced to play this really horrible game."* But on the other hand, she couldn't introduce herself as Chika, either. She could say they went to the same school, but that was Chika, not Pechka. Even if she didn't mean it as a lie, it would end up being one. If he were to search for Pechka and her perfect lunches at school, she wouldn't be there.

She replied that she always cooked for her friends, and when they ate it, they'd say it was really good. Ninomiya laughed. "Well, of course! Anyone who didn't think so couldn't be human!" Pechka smiled, but inside, she felt despondent.

Then the third day arrived. That evening, she would be summoned into the game again, where she would have to survive for three more days. She hated this. She wanted to cry. She wanted to give up. At the very least, she wanted to confess everything about her situation to him right there and then. Even if he couldn't help, he could offer sympathy, at least. But despite her desires, there was no way she could tell him anything. If she did, she would die on the spot.

So she talked about herself. Not Chika Tatehara, and not the magical girl Pechka, but a fictitious girl who attended a high school in the neighborhood, liked cooking, and enjoyed baseball. Her mother had taught her to cook. Her mother was far better at it. Recently, a cat had pooped in their yard, and her grampa had gotten angry about it. She even concocted a story about her friend slipping on a banana peel, like something out of a manga. She had gone to karaoke and input the wrong song numbers into the machine, but by coincidence, they had known all the songs, so they'd sung them to the end. Ninomiya laughed at her made-up stories of failure, and Pechka dammed up her sadness and pain with a smile.

He finished the lunch, thanked her with his hands together like he always did, and returned the box. When he handed it back to her, their pinkie fingers brushed. Ninomiya wasn't bothered by it at all. He just ran off. "See you later!"

Pechka studied the tip of her pinkie, touched the finger to her other hand, and squeezed it.

☆ Shadow Gale

Kanoe was getting lost in her thoughts more often. Or, more accurately, she was just zoning out and not even trying to hide her contemplation. That was something she'd never done before, and her parents and older brother were concerned. But when they asked if something was on her mind, she would grin back at them, saying it was nothing to worry about—and that was what really made them worry. They asked Mamori about her, too, but she couldn't give them an answer. If it were possible, she would have loved to tell them, *"The young mistress is a magical girl, and right now, she's been forced into playing a game where failure equals death."*

Kanoe was still mulling over something. That was fine. There were plenty of things Mamori would have liked to think about, too. But she chose certain places for her pondering. If she wanted to think, she would go to her own room. She wouldn't occupy someone else's room like she owned the place the way Kanoe would. She wouldn't put wine and crackers on a tray, barge in, and have her snack on someone else's study desk. She also wouldn't drop the crackers on the desk and scatter crumbs.

Mamori stood up, raised the blinds, and opened the window. The autumn wind at night was more than cool; it was rather chilly. The stale air swept outside, while the fresh breeze wafted in. There was a swath of green grass outside the window, and the dusk had dyed it dark-purplish. A tall hedge surrounded the yard, and the chirping of the insects sounded pleasant to the ears. Mamori had heard that they'd bought some pine crickets just to release them here. They were apparently a few thousand yen per cricket, but she wanted to believe that the story had been exaggerated in the telling.

She left the window, returned to the bed, and sat down. Glancing over, she saw that Kanoe was still on the swivel chair, lost in thought. Mamori wished she would at least think in her own room. The whole Totoyama family lived on Hitokouji lands, and Mamori's room was in the Hitokoujis' mansion, so it made it hard to complain when Kanoe marched in whenever she wanted.

But that chair was different. It was European-made, bought for thirty-five thousand yen from an order catalog. She intended to keep on using it for the next twenty or thirty years. It was wonderful and comfortable to sit in, and Mamori had bought it with money she'd saved over some time. It was clearly her own personal property. Even if it was inside the Hitokouji estate, Kanoe should have no right to use it.

"Would you please at least give me back my chair?" Mamori said.

"You have something on your mind, too, don't you?" Kanoe returned her question with another question. But she was right that Mamori was thinking about something, too. She'd been ruminating a lot, and she'd never been able to come up with any answers, either. How and what would you do to take one candy away from Cherna Mouse? Mamori had no idea. She didn't even know what the point of doing it was in the first place.

During the event at the end of the last logout day, Cherna Mouse had died. Detec Bell and Melville had immediately tried to revive her, but mouth-to-mouth and chest compressions hadn't done anything, and even the recovery medicine hadn't worked. They couldn't revive her. The cause of death was a heart attack.

As Fal had explained it, the one who held the smallest amount of magical candy would lose. The loss conditions were in the terms "smallest" and "one," both of which had to be fulfilled. Otherwise no one would lose. Pfle had guessed that if there was more than one person with the lowest figure, then nothing would happen, and Fal had said that was correct. If there were two or more magical girls holding the lowest number, then they could get through the event without anyone losing.

Everyone had cooperated in the reallocation of candy, and Pfle had double-checked. So they had managed to get through the event—or so they had thought for the instant before Cherna Mouse fell and Fal called her name out. When they had picked up her magical phone to check it, the number displayed there was one fewer than that of the other girls.

Some began to accuse Pfle of failing to check the candy numbers properly, but many others denied that.

In her duel with Cherna Mouse, Pfle had lost her wheelchair, so she got around by riding Shadow Gale piggyback. Shadow Gale had actually been the one walking around so Pfle could check the candy numbers of the magical girls sitting around the fountain. And that wasn't all she was doing. She'd been looking at their magical phones. She was certain their numbers had all been the same. There was no way she could have failed to notice that one was wrong.

The other magical girls also gave testimony to Pfle's innocence. They'd all followed the order to keep an eye on their neighbors, either because they couldn't trust one another or because they wanted to. To Cherna Mouse's right had been Detec Bell, and to her left, Melville. Shadow Gale had confirmed that the candy numbers on both their screens had matched the number on Cherna Mouse's phone.

So then why had Cherna Mouse died? Why had she ended up with one fewer than the others?

Mamori came to no answers.

You could use a magical phone to transfer candy. But if anyone had done that after everyone's candy was arranged, the phones' beeps would have exposed them. It would have been possible *before* all the candy was sorted out. While they'd been arranging the candy, the square had been filled with the *beep, beep, beep, beep* of enchanted electronics. But it would have been pointless to meddle with the candy numbers at that point. Pfle and Shadow Gale had checked them all afterward, and Cherna's neighbors on either side had done the same. If the numbers had been off, it would have been caught.

Had someone manipulated the phones with magic? That couldn't be done, either. You could physically smash the devices, but even after disassembly, it was impossible to rig anything there or set anything inside. If you tried to control a phone from the outside using magic, it would just break. Shadow Gale had already verified this personally.

"Cherna Mouse's candy..." Mamori's thoughts spilled from her mouth.

Kanoe pulled a math notebook out of a drawer in the study desk, flicked off the pen cap with her thumb, and smoothly wrote out the names of all the magical girls, the parties they were affiliated with, and the magic powers they had.

"That's my notebook...my pen...," Mamori protested.

"Yeah. I'm using them."

- Party A
  Pfle: high-powered wheelchair
  Shadow Gale: mechanical modification

- Party B
  Clantail: transforming the lower half of her body into an animal
  Rionetta: controlling dolls

Nonako Miyokata: making allies of animals
Pechka: creating delicious food

- Party C (Cherna Mouse's party)
  Detec Bell: conversing with buildings—can't use it in
  the game (sat right of Cherna Mouse)
  Melville: camouflage (sat left of Cherna mouse)
  Lapis Lazuline: teleporting to location of her gem
  Cherna Mouse: making herself big (victim)

- Party D
  Nokko: transmitting her emotions
  @Meow-Meow: capturing items within her talismans
  Genopsyko Yumenoshima: invincible suit (only her
  phone participated)

The postmortem breakdown was detailed with more information than Mamori had anticipated. "How is this so thorough? You've got the magic of people you've never even talked to listed here."

"Because unlike you with your hunting task, as the one in charge of exploration, I've come to know more people. After that great scuffle in the square, I immediately went asking around. Though in the end the killer was presumed to be that samurai girl, we were still victims. Our ally had been killed and her items stolen. I'm sure none of them wanted to draw suspicion by trying to hide their abilities and failing."

"And can we believe this information?" asked Mamori.

"When I asked each of these people, they were within earshot of their fellow party members. If they had lied, their allies would have reacted somehow. Even if they didn't directly accuse that person and ask why they were lying, they'd have had some kind of tell. But if someone is lying about her magic even to her own party... then that's something else." If someone were lying to even her own party about her magic, that one would be the culprit.

"Have you figured out who did it? Like does one of the girls have powers that could have manipulated Cherna Mouse's amount of candy?"

"I don't care about that."

"You don't? But—"

"I thought I told you: I don't need proof. All I need to know about is character. This memo is ultimately just an expression of goodwill toward you. I'm not going to try to deduct the culprit's identity based on opportunity or motive. But you're different, aren't you? So I'm sure you'll find this useful."

Kanoe shoved the notebook at Mamori, scooped up the stuffed bear that sat on the side of the bed, and plopped down on the chair again. So apparently, all that thinking hadn't been about how the culprit had removed a candy from Cherna Mouse's inventory. Mamori was privately disappointed, but she kept her expression stiff to hide her feelings from Kanoe. She plopped onto the bed and then lay down.

Using that knowledge of all of the girls' abilities, and also taking into consideration the in-game items, Mamori tried to come up with a way someone could have removed that candy from Cherna Mouse's magical phone. But she couldn't. In fact, it was impossible. Simply destroying the phone was one thing, but bending its functionality to your whims was impossible. Messing up the display or silencing the beeping just couldn't be done.

If Mamori were forced to come up with the most likely suspect, it would be herself. Her magical ability to modify machines was broad in scope, and even if she couldn't tamper with the displays or the noises they made, she could have come up with some incredible way to remove that one candy. However, Mamori knew that Shadow Gale was not the culprit. She hadn't done it.

But—there was a *but*. Though Mamori knew she was innocent, the others wouldn't know that for certain. She had plenty of motive to do it, too, after Cherna Mouse had beaten them in a duel the other day. If they began to suspect her, things could get bad.

"I didn't do it," Mamori said out loud.

"I know that."

Well, Kanoe *would* say that. Though to anyone else, it might appear as if she were trying to cover for her own, Kanoe would at least advocate on her behalf—whether or not that would work.

"It's all right," said Kanoe. "They're not going to suspect you—"

"Uh, I think most people would find me the most suspicious of all."

"—since I told them your magic is creating tanks." Mamori stared at Kanoe, shocked, and Kanoe returned her gaze with a calm expression. "Well, it's less suspicious, isn't it?"

"But even before that..." Mamori pushed her upper body off the bed. "We still haven't found who killed Masked Wonder and stole her items."

"Indeed."

Masked Wonder had been killed and her items robbed. The Miracle Coin, one of the items she'd been holding on to, hadn't been in any of their phones, but someone still had it. The item was at 1 (1), so it had to be in someone's device.

Mamori felt like these two incidents were similar. With both the Miracle Coin and Cherna Mouse, the impossible had happened, and the magical phones were connected to the mystery. "...The same culprit?" Mamori suggested.

"That's possible."

What about motive? The reason behind Masked Wonder's murder was probably the theft of the Miracle Coin. But while it was a rare item, would you kill someone for something only ambiguously useful? It was true that the deadly stakes hadn't yet been revealed, but this game was full of just and true magical girls.

And Cherna Mouse... Had it just been because she'd been an obstacle? Cherna Mouse's role had been to chase away any parties that would try to set foot in their hunting spots. So it made sense that she'd be an obstacle to playing the game.

The motives for the both of these were related to the game. Setting aside Masked Wonder's death, by the time Cherna Mouse had been killed, the goal of everyone had already changed from finishing the game to escaping, which would be facilitated by playing.

Cherna Mouse's party had been selfish and inconsiderate, but not enough to kill her for it. None of them knew what kinds of quests might come next, and without Cherna Mouse, they might run into a monster they couldn't beat. If the Evil King turned out to be three hundred feet tall and weighed 150,000 tons, then their survival would have depended on Cherna winning.

But someone had wanted Cherna Mouse gone nonetheless...or had they? What if Cherna Mouse hadn't been the target, and she'd just happened to be the one to die? Or...

"...Something just occurred to me that I really don't want to consider, but...may I?"

"Go ahead."

"This is all the master's work."

"And why do you think that?"

"I think that maybe both the theft of the Miracle Coin and the interference in that event were attempts to prevent us completing the game. The master has teased us with the hope that we can escape if we win, but they're secretly meddling in things to prevent us from succeeding. Can't you just imagine them laughing as they watch us tremble in our boots? Since the master has pulled us into the game world, that means their magic clearly has to do with machines or computers or something like that, right? I'm sure they can do anything they want within that realm. So wouldn't they be able to manipulate the magical phones and all that?" If that were true, then things were bleak. The master was both the sponsor and the manager of that world, so if they were serious about obstructing the players, the magical girls wouldn't stand a chance. If the master wanted to torture them to death, it would be done, and if the master wanted to kill them all on the spot, it would happen.

"You don't have to consider the idea that the master is the culprit."

"Why not?"

"Because if that's what the master wants," Kanoe explained, "then we'll be helpless to resist. We'll all die. There's no avoiding that."

"So are you saying that we shouldn't resist?"

"No."

It was a bleak idea. What's more, nothing else seemed likely to Mamori.

But even after all of that, Kanoe's full lips were curved in a faint smile. "If that's what the master wants to do, then there's nothing we can do about it. They're capable of locking sixteen magical girls inside a game world and maintaining total control over our lives and deaths. Their magic is powerful, so there's no point in thinking about how to kill them or make them surrender."

"You're saying to give up?"

"Let me finish." Placing the stuffed bear on her lap, Kanoe spun the swivel chair around to face Mamori. "Even if we were to pursue the possibility that the master has come to torment and kill us, we wouldn't be able to resolve the issue, so we won't consider that avenue. I presume completing the game will solve that. I'll expend efforts on the possibility that one of the magical girls participating in this game is malicious and has used some means to steal the coin from Masked Wonder and manipulate Cherna Mouse's candy."

"So that's that, then?" At first glance, it seemed like a proactive approach, choosing to ignore the most probable avenue because it was impossible to resolve even if you racked your brain and pursuing only the less likely option instead. But it was still just avoiding reality.

"If the master is the culprit," Kanoe continued, "then there's nothing we can do, so we should give up. There's no way we can fight the master from within the game as players, anyway. Even if we were to challenge them, it would be best put off until afterward. Besides, the theory that the culprit is someone other than the master isn't all that preposterous. One could take that view as well. The master has made a challenging and malicious game, but they've also prepared some escape keys that the more canny individuals can deduce. Such was the case with having multiple people hold the lowest value of candy, and also with how the monster encyclopedia was sold in the town near the monsters that reflect projectile weapons. The master is the type who offers a way out and then laughs at those who fail to notice this and die. Stealing items via physical force and manipulating the candy numbers from the outside are inconsistent with the master's character. Naturally, one would assume that someone other than the master is acting here. Well, I would."

The stuffed bear bulged. Kanoe's arms were wrapped around its neck, squeezing. Her smile was fixed as ever, but she was clenching the bear so hard, its figure distorted. "The culprit will pay." Mamori realized that Kanoe was angry.

Kanoe never forgave people who caused harm to her own—and "her own" did not mean her immediate family or blood relations. It referred to the people close to her generally.

When the two of them had just started high school, some people had called Mamori a parasite on Kanoe's butt. When the rumor reached even her, the target, she figured it had really been going around. Those who had gone to their middle school would never have dared to gossip like that, but a lot of people at their high school had come in from other schools.

Those girls who had gotten their kicks badmouthing Mamori were away from school for a week after that. By the time they came back, they'd transformed into good girls who would never belittle anyone. That was probably related to why they blanched and trembled whenever Kanoe got near them.

Masked Wonder had been an ally.

Mamori laced her fingers, placed her hands in her lap, and looked down.

Masked Wonder had been a real heroine of justice. When she saw someone who was hurt, she rushed to their aid with zero suspicion. When she believed she was in the right, she even stood up to an opponent over thirty yards tall without hesitation. Shadow Gale had been skeptical of her, finding it fishy that someone would introduce themselves as "justice," but Masked Wonder had expended every effort to do the right thing at all times. She had lacked any cynicism or sarcasm and always dealt with things sincerely.

Masked Wonder's head had been crushed by a rock, and then she had died. It was horrible that she'd met her end that way.

Biting her lip, Mamori lifted her head and looked over at Kanoe. That smile was still on her face. The stuffed bear wasn't bulging anymore. "I will observe character," said Kanoe, "and you think up method. This is how we'll find the culprit."

Still biting her lip, Mamori nodded.

☆ Detec Bell

They buried Cherna Mouse's body at the edge of town. They placed the sunflower seeds she'd loved in her grave, saving one extra for once they'd filled the hole. That seed sat on top of the mound of earth as a grave marker. Her giant sunflower seeds were, of course, not something that really existed. Cherna Mouse had said they were a part of her costume. They had also been edible, and whenever she'd had a free moment, she had nibbled on them. She was the only one of them who hadn't bought rations at the shop. Lapis Lazuline had envied her for that.

Now she was sniffling.

Detec Bell glanced over to Melville, thinking of calling out to her to discuss what would happen next. Melville's eyes were on her. The words Detec Bell had been about to say died halfway from her throat.

Melville said quietly, "Ah'm taekin' me leave o' this pairty."

"...What?" said Detec Bell.

Melville was even more detached than usual. "There be a vill'n among's, an' Ah cannae fathom who. Cherna's slain, an' Ah've no trust fer ennyone. Ah'm loathe t'leave ye, but Ah must."

"'One of us is a bad guy, and I don't know who it is. They killed Cherna. I can't trust nobody no more, so there's no point in having a party. I feel bad, but I'm leaving,' is what Melvy is sayin'... Wait, Melvy!" Lazuline wiped her tears and snot with a sleeve and put her hand on Melville's shoulder. "You're leavin' the party?! How can ya say that?! This is the part where everyone bands together! It'd be so sad if ya left the party now!"

"Y'wish to go wi' me? If ye follow, Ah shan't tell ye nay."

"I'm not goin'! But I'm totally against ya leavin', Melvy!"

Melville swiped aside Lazuline's hand. Lazuline tried to leap on her anyway, but Melville hopped lightly over the sunflower seed grave marker, putting it between them. Lazuline, unwilling to trample the grave marker, stumbled forward.

Detec Bell tried to find the right words. She couldn't let Melville withdraw from the party. *If there were just something I could say to make her rethink this. If she could just stay with us,* she thought, but she couldn't come up with anything. "Does this mean you don't trust me?" The words that came out of her mouth were horribly cold and dry. Detec Bell licked her lips. They felt parched and rough. No moisture at all. "You won't stop Lazuline from following, but you're leaving the party. That means you can't trust me, doesn't it?"

"Listen..." Melville's body faded. Her face, clothes, longbow, harpoons, everything turned the color of the wasteland dirt, blending into it. "'Ere's no need fer such grievance. Dinnae trouble yerself wi' the question o' trust. Y'only must keep gaun yer own way. Ah'll be taekin' retribution fer Cherna an' then taekin' me leave."

"'You don't have to take it so badly,'" Lazuline translated. "'I'm going to go search for the one who killed Cherny and get revenge. You guys just aim to complete the game on your own,' she says."

"But it had to be the master who killed Cherna, right?" said Detec Bell. Clearly, no one else could have done it. Not only had Cherna Mouse's magical phone displayed the same number as everyone else's before the time limit was up, it had even displayed the same number *after* the time ran out. Detec Bell had been right beside her, watching, so she knew that for a fact. Cherna had fallen and dropped her magical phone, and once the phone had hit the ground, for some reason, it had one fewer candy. That sort of feat was impossible using either magic or items. And that impossible thing had, in fact, happened. There was only one person who could have pulled that off: the master.

"That event was designed to produce a loser, but Pfle found a way out and went for it," said Detec Bell. "That made the master angry, so they twisted the rules of the game. They made one of us lose, just according to their original plan, and then took away a magical candy from her so that we couldn't complain."

"Nay. Recall ye Fal's reaction. He 'os well aware."

"'That's not right. Please, think back on how Fal reacted. He knew about it,'" Lazuline interpreted.

"'Twas no fault o' th' rules but a boon to th' plaeyers."

"'That wasn't a hole in the rules. I think that was a way out for the players.'"

"Methinks 'twas pairt o' th' master's designs. No cause fer anger."

"'The master originally planned that in. It was the right answer. There's no reason to be angry.'"

"Ah had a fearf'l notion that sommon 'os laughin'."

"'I had this horrible feeling then. Someone was laughing at us.'"

"When Cherna fell. Sommon 'os laughin'."

"'When Cherna fell, someone was laughing.'"

"An' Genopsyko says 'ere be a traetor."

"'And there's also that message Genopsyko left us. She told us there's a traitor.'"

"Tha's the lass wha' did the deed...an' I havte faend 'em."

"'That person is the culprit. I'm going to find them.'"

Even as Melville spoke and Lazuline translated, Melville was fading into the background. Eventually, her form and her voice disappeared entirely. Lazuline was waiting to translate the next part, but Melville didn't say anything more.

"Ah...Melvy's gone!" Lazuline ran around the grave marker, flailing her arms, but all she swiped through was air. She never touched anything. Melville had made herself invisible and left.

Detec Bell turned on her magical phone and opened up the party composition screen. The party members' names were all registered there: Detec Bell, Lapis Lazuline, and Cherna Mouse. Melville's name was already gone. Fal had said parties were easy to join and easy to leave. It really was that easy.

"Lazuline."

"What? Is there some way we can call her back?"

"Let me see your phone for a second."

"Okay. What for, though?" Lapis Lazuline asked as she handed Detec Bell her magical phone.

It looked just the same as any other. Detec Bell tapped the heart-shaped screen to operate it, moving to the wallpaper screen and the address book. "Whoops, wrong screen." She went back a screen and brought up the party formation. It was just the same here as in Detec Bell's magical phone. Three names were all listed there, but not Melville's. Clicking on Cherna Mouse's name, she selected REMOVE, and then only two names remained. Apparently, the survivors had to remove the dead from their party.

Detec Bell handed the phone back to Lazuline and then tugged down her deerstalker cap. She was liable to start crying, and she didn't want Lazuline to see.

"Melvy…she said she was goin' to search for the culprit. I wonder if there really is one."

Was Lazuline talking to her, or just muttering to herself? When Detec Bell didn't reply, she didn't react, so it was probably the latter.

The detective clenched her teeth, the corners of her mouth turning downward. Her feelings of frustration, oppression, and helplessness were growing. She had believed that as long as they had Cherna Mouse, they'd be all right, no matter what happened. Cherna Mouse had been so prideful, too, saying that with her there, they could protect everyone. Though she'd abused her strength to drive off the others, she'd still been a reliable ally. And dependable Cherna had been killed in such an unwarranted manner, through means that had nothing at all to do with her strength.

Detec Bell was the party leader, but Cherna Mouse had been the real cornerstone of their party—and the one who'd been giving her orders had been Melville. Without their cornerstone, Melville had gone, and Detec Bell was left behind.

It might also have seemed like Lazuline had been abandoned, too—but it wasn't the same with her. Right as Melville had left, she'd invited Lazuline. When she'd said that she wouldn't stop

Lazuline if she would accompany her, that had meant she was okay being in a party with Lazuline. In other words, that meant the reason Melville had left was Detec Bell.

Did Melville not trust her? Or did she consider her unnecessary? Whichever it was, thinking about it made her want to cry. Detec Bell had been their leader in name, but she hadn't particularly achieved anything. They hadn't managed to unlock even a single area. The other parties had done all of that.

Her magic was useless inside the game. But she still had experience working as a detective. She had the knowledge she'd gained from reading mystery novels. She'd believed that even if she couldn't use her magic here, she could still be useful. However, once they'd started the game, she'd been unable to unlock a single area, and she lacked any authority as their leader. Cherna Mouse and Melville had just ignored her instructions instead.

"If there *is* someone out there who killed Cherny," said Lazuline, "I ain't lettin' them get away with this! It's super-dangerous to have someone like that runnin' free without ever gettin' punished, right?"

Detec Bell observed her. Lapis Lazuline had gone from raging to frightened to restless. Melville had invited her to come along. Right before leaving their party, she'd invited Lazuline. Detec Bell glared at Lazuline from underneath her deerstalker cap.

The girl in blue smacked her right hand to her chest and assured her, "But don't you fret. As long as I, Lapis Lazuline, am here, you'll be safe, Bell."

Not long after that, they got their break from the game, and Detec Bell returned to reality and her life as Shinobu Hioka. No longer her magical-girl self, she was human again, but she was still smoldering on the inside.

She punched the wall of the apartment building and immediately called the office and requested ten days off. She dreaded that her boss would either tell her she didn't have to come back and fire her, or just berate her in his thick voice, asking her what the hell she was thinking. So she gave her request and immediately turned off her phone.

Shinobu pulled out her magical device and searched the Internet. She'd memorized the area code listed in Lazuline's phone's address book. She looked it up and immediately identified the name of the town in question. Writing it down on a memo pad, she then searched for the train schedule.

Detec Bell couldn't use her power inside the game—but she could use it in real life. First, Lapis Lazuline. Detec Bell would search for the region she worked in as a magical girl in real life and find out her real identity using the same methods she'd used investigating Magical Daisy.

She would work in reality and gather information in reality. If, as Melville said, one of the magical girls was in communication with the enemy, then Detec Bell would find out who. If she discovered someone to be a totally innocent magical girl with no secrets at all, that was also useful information. She just had to add to the list of people she could trust, one by one.

Yes, Lapis Lazuline came first. One of their party had been killed, and another of them had left, and yet she still acted so happy-go-lucky. Was that just the kind of person she was, or did she keep a secret that allowed her to feel that way? Detec Bell would find out.

☆ Pechka

When they went back into the game, they began in the wasteland area. No matter where they were upon logout, they'd return in the wasteland area. Simply put, it seemed they would be forced back to their starting points every single time. When Pechka checked the locations of her fellow party members on the map, she got the feeling they were in the same positions they had been the last time they came.

The wasteland hadn't changed at all. The sky was solid blue, the sun glared abnormally hot, the earth was barren, and the crumbling buildings towered high. Occasionally, a wind would gust through, sweeping up red-brown-colored dirt and sand, and every time, Pechka squeezed her eyes shut.

Pechka met with Clantail first. She thought she saw a doll on the horizon, and then suddenly, Clantail was in front of her. Though she'd lost to Pfle's wheelchair in a contest of speed, when Clantail sprinted at full velocity, she was much faster than the animals her transformations were based off.

"It's been a while," said Pechka.

"Yeah." Clantail was as taciturn as always. She turned away from Pechka and knelt. Pechka swung a leg over her back and wrapped her arms around Clantail's stomach—not her animal stomach, her human one. She recalled when they had first met, when she'd been bundled up in spider's silk, trembling and slung over Clantail's back. Back then, Clantail had seemed like a monster that had scared the wits out of her. But now that they were fighting dragons, Pechka was used to it. It was interesting how the animal part she sat on and the human part she gripped with her arms had different body temperatures.

"Clantail…"

"Hmm?"

"Your human and animal parts are different temperatures, huh?"

Clantail didn't reply. When Pechka tilted around to look at her face, she found it was stiff, her cheeks pink. Maybe she'd made Clantail angry? Just being more familiar with her didn't mean Pechka could be so cheeky with her. She was flustered and about to apologize when Clantail suddenly jumped. Pechka lost her balance and clung on tight, and when she looked behind them, she saw a big rock. They must have jumped over that. She'd nearly been shaken off, though that might have been a coincidence. Maybe she had made Clantail angry after all.

"Um…," Pechka began. "Thank you for giving me a ride every time, when we meet up."

"No…" Clantail's voice became quieter. "Thank you…for making food all the time…" She spoke so quietly, the sound of her hooves drowned out her voice, but Pechka still managed to catch that somehow. Did that appreciation mean Clantail wasn't mad?

Clantail lifted her spear, pointing ahead. "Over there."

Someone was waving. It was Nonako Miyokata. She was with the dragon she'd made her friend last time. "*Ha-ha-ha!* At last, the time has come! Long time no see!"

Nonako took Clantail's hand and shook it and then shook Pechka's so vigorously that she dragged her off Clantail's back. Even once she was down, Nonako didn't let go of her hand, swinging her around and spinning in a circle. "*Ha-ha-ha-ha-ha-ha-ha-ha-ha!* I'm so excited!"

Nonako was clearly giddy and, once she was done swinging Pechka every which way, finally let go. She'd gotten herself so worked up, her shoulders were heaving. Her dragon was watching her with concern. "Oh…I got a little too excited…*un peu*…"

"Are you all right?" asked Pechka.

"I'm fine, I'm fine! No *problème*. Come on, let's go. If we dawdle even a little, that obnoxious doll girl will start whining."

The three of them all started running in the direction of Rio-netta's icon. Even as they ran, Nonako occasionally laughed, fooled around, and played with her dragon.

She was making a deliberate attempt to act more cheerful. Pechka was, too. Clantail had always been the quiet type, but now she was smiling at Nonako's antics. The way things had ended during their last session, there was no way they could start things off on a merry note this time. But now they were all putting on this enthusiastic act. It was like they were hoping that if they acted as if this were a little joke, then maybe it really would turn into just a joke.

While dark thoughts gripped Pechka, they reached Rionetta. Her arms were folded, and she was steadily tapping on her forearm with her index finger. "You're late!" She was the only one not trying to hide her bad mood. "Why have you made me wait so long? I would very much appreciate it if you could explain just what you were up to that required such dawdling."

"See!" cawed Nonako. "Just like I said, *hein*? She'd still be whining even if we came at Mach 1 speed."

"Oh? What was that? Speaking poorly of me behind my back? What fabulous adaptive capability you have. I'm quite impressed by your mastery of Japanese culture."

"I was just speaking objective fact. If facts count as talking behind someone's back, then you're the one with the *problème*."

"You can never keep your mouth shut."

"Oh, then I shall try to do better." They were already at it with no signs of tiring.

Clantail didn't say anything; she just turned away from them and galloped off to the wasteland town. Still griping and sniping at each other, Rionetta and Nonako ran after her, while the dragon flew along behind them. Pechka was about to follow, but then she suddenly stopped.

She sniffed. *Sniff, sniff.* And two more sniffs—she could smell something. It was faint, but there was a floral scent in the air, something that seemed incongruous in the wasteland. Not a rare flower. If she had to say, it was common. Yes, this flower was...

"Pechkaaa...ou'll get le...hiiind..."

She was jerked back to reality. Looking off, she could see that the other three girls and the dragon had come to a halt in the distance and were turned back toward her. Nonako Miyokata's hands were cupped around her mouth, but she was still so far away, Pechka could only catch bits of what she was saying.

Flustered, Pechka dashed off.

"They went thataway! One red, one green!" Rionetta said, luring the enemy dragons in as Clantail raced past to strike one with her spear. There was the crackle and flash of a lightning strike, burning the red dragon black before it collided with a cliff.

They were still hunting dragons in the subterranean area. They'd done this so many times already, they'd generally come to grips with the creatures' attack patterns. They were now able to grind effectively, and they used up very little of the recovery medicine Pechka carried.

Just as Rionetta had said before the last logout, the lack of Cherna Mouse's obstruction made a big difference. Their worries that Melville or Lapis Lazuline would be keeping watch even with Cherna Mouse gone were unfounded. They were able to move freely between hunting grounds. Detec Bell's team had been occupying the dragon treasury, so they went on killing all three colors one after another to grind for the items and magical candy.

"I'd like to get a newer weapon," said Rionetta, "if you don't mind. Our current weapons are decent enough against dragons, but there is the future to consider. Whatever you buy at the subterranean shop is all so expensive. It's quite the concern."

"Can we roll some more *R*?" asked Nonako. "Also, if there are any weapons or armor *mon bébé* can equip, I'd like to buy them."

Pechka chimed in, too. "If you have the first aid kit item, you can put a dozen recovery medicines inside. I'd like to be able to carry more of those around."

They bought some more items, set up their equipment, and killed some more dragons. Afterward, Pechka made their meal.

As Rionetta, Nonako, and Clantail's tail all squirmed in ecstasy, they ate. From rolling more *R*s, they got spoons, forks, plates, and bowls. With not just their food but their cutlery upgraded as well, it turned into a real, full-blown meal.

In a way, all this fighting, arming themselves with items and equipment, and eating good food was just an escape from reality. They had to keep moving, keep running, or they would surely lose their minds. Cherna's unwarranted death was more than enough reason for them to give up on the game, but even so, right now, they had no choice but to continue playing. They could only close their eyes to the inconceivable results that could fall upon them at any time and make themselves believe that it wouldn't happen anymore.

They just had to keep moving. They explored every inch of the subterranean area map and searched for hints. The underground region was big enough to span the entirety of the wasteland and the grasslands areas, and there were a lot of places to investigate. Doing that while also hunting dragons made progress slow and stalling.

"There was a message on a different-colored rock wall that said there's a dragon king," Pechka informed them.

"A king?" said Nonako. "I suppose it must drop lots of bon-bons?"

"It says the space around its throne is bordered in red," added Rionetta.

As was clear from the fact that they hadn't managed even one area unlock quest, this party was not good at solving puzzles. Pechka was noncombat personnel, but that didn't mean she was the one in charge of intellectual labor; Rionetta and Nonako just moaned in the face of cipher texts; and from Clantail's manner, it seemed she'd never even considered that sort of thing to be her job.

They gathered a bunch of hints that they couldn't even be sure were helpful. *The dragons have a king. The space around its throne is bordered in red. Under the city. Thirty-four, forty-one, twenty-six. Water and a big shield. Glasses of bygone days. What's gained from death. Leave it to the specialist.* There was no way they could derive any answers from all that. This was exactly why their policy had been to leave it to others and allow the other parties to unlock areas. They collected hints just in case while they focused on their main task: hunting dragons.

"This is taking a rather long time, though," Rionetta murmured during their meal.

"More of your whining about others being late? You're always going on about time, *hein*?"

Rionetta ignored Nonako's jab and continued. "Isn't it about time that someone discovered the next area? I believe so far, they've been unlocked at a rather faster clip."

"Oh, you're right," agreed Pechka. "It has been a while."

"I don't want to linger so long in such a damp, dark place. How thoughtless of them. Oh, Pechka? Whatever are you using as a thickener in these Salisbury steaks?"

"I think it might be bread crumbs."

"Simply brilliant," Rionetta said.

"Now that you mention it, it *has* been a long time," Nonako said.

"Numpties like you never do understand unless it's spelled out for them, hmm?"

"*Excusez-moi?*"

"I was complimenting you, saying that you understand when things are explained to you. So what are you so cross about?"

"Um," Pechka interrupted, "there's more food, if anyone would like seconds."

"*Donnez-moi!* Please!"

"I shall partake."

Pechka served some to Nonako, some to Rionetta, and some to Clantail, who silently held her bowl out, then added some to her own bowl while she was at it. After that, she just spooned food into her mouth. Pechka was kind of like their mom now.

A few hours later, things started happening. Clantail's magical phone sounded its ringtone, and everyone froze. Clantail checked her phone and showed the other three the screen. It displayed her inbox, with a message from Pfle. The text was simple. It read,

Discovered area unlock quest. But completing it alone would be challenging. Help requested.

Rionetta said, "Seems we can finally carry on to the next area," smiling in satisfaction.

☆ Nokko

They hadn't been able to figure out why Cherna Mouse had died. At the very least, Nokko hadn't been involved, so that meant someone else had done it. There was some panicking about how maybe the master had done it, but based off what they had seen of the master's character thus far, it seemed unlikely that they would interfere in a way that ignored the rules to arbitrarily put the players at a disadvantage.

Cherna Mouse must have been hated by and alienated from the rest of them. A magical girl shutting the other parties out of the good hunting grounds was bound to incur dislike. Cherna Mouse may have been doing that under orders, but she was the one recognized for the act. Besides, you could also say it was her ability, or rather, her body, that allowed them to engage in that monopolistic behavior in the first place.

And her victory in her duel with Pfle had made that clear. The wheelchair tank, constructed from so much material, hadn't been able to beat Cherna. Nobody could beat her, and as long as she was around, Detec Bell's party would have continued to monopolize hunting grounds.

In order to stop their domination of the hunting grounds, Cherna Mouse had to go. However, no one would have used that as a basis to kill such a powerful player in an event. All their lives were hanging on completing the game, so if they were left with no more tanks, then they would all be in trouble. It was a horrible idea to kill someone over a petty squabble.

So then who had done it?

None of the players would have benefited from killing her. And it hadn't been a case of flying into a rage and doing it without thinking. There was also no reason for the master to have killed her. Nokko knew that she herself was not the culprit. There wasn't anyone who could have done it.

The entire incident seemed extremely ominous to Nokko, and @Meow-Meow had to feel the same way. It was the sort of incident that could make you fall into despair, if worst came to worst. But despite that, @Meow-Meow was hunting dragons, gathering hints, and searching for Genopsyko besides. She had given the other parties her number and told them to contact her if they saw the missing girl.

"There must be some reason," said @Meow-Meow. "Some kind of situation she can't get out of, and she just can't come to us."

"Yes…of course," Nokko agreed. She felt like @Meow-Meow was trying to convince herself of that, too. But still, she figured her friend seemed more positive, which was at least better than the stupor she'd been in before.

They hunted dragons, gathered candy, and bought equipment

and items. Nokko surmised the other parties had to be doing the same thing. She didn't want to participate, but still, she couldn't see anything else she should do. This game was the only place for them to vent their feelings using their magical-girl powers, so Nokko hit the dragons with all her resentment and indignation.

That was when they got the message from Pfle.

Discovered area unlock quest. But completing it alone would be challenging. Help requested.

The message also said that Pfle's party would be waiting for a while in the subterranean town. So if they could help, please come.

"That's what it says. So what will we do?" asked Nokko.

"Of course we help them." @Meow-Meow was filled with intrepid spirit, her eyes shining with the light of her unbending will. But considering how uneasy she had to be in their situation and how unsteady she had been, all her overflowing energy now seemed off. Even if she did fit the standard magical-girl archetype of standing up in times of crises, trusted her allies, never faltering, and never giving in—even if she was just that sort of noble and righteous magical girl—it would have been normal for her to feel more tortured by feelings of helplessness.

Did @Meow-Meow know something? Before she'd snapped out of her daze, she'd been muttering to herself. Did she have some knowledge that enabled her to face all of this?

The town in the subterranean area looked pretty similar to the other towns. The old buildings were made of stone. There was no one in the streets and no one living there. There were windows, but no glass panes. All the messages in the shop were pure pleasantry. If there was any difference at all, it was that it was far more humid here, with a moldy smell on top of that. This was something Nokko could say of the subterranean area as a whole, and she wouldn't want to live there.

There were a number of magical girls at the meet-up spot. The centaur, shrine maiden, chef, and doll were Clantail's party of four. The shrine maiden and the doll were glaring at each other. Every time Nokko saw them, they were fighting. Were those two all right?

Detec Bell's party was there, too. Lacking Cherna Mouse, it was now Lapis Lazuline and Detec Bell. Then there was Melville… Nokko looked around for her and found her sitting on a rock alone, away from the party.

Shadow Gale was carrying Pfle on her back. Nokko and @Meow-Meow approached Pfle first, calling out to her.

"Hello," said Pfle. "Good of you to come."

"Your wheelchair still not fixed?" asked @Meow-Meow.

"It's not quite that it needs fixing. Rather, it needs remaking. Have you acquired any chairs through R?"

"I'm sorry," said Nokko. "We haven't been buying any Rs."

"I see… I've been asking everyone here, but no one has a chair. If you happen to acquire one, do allow us to have it. I'll make it worth your while."

That Pfle was without her wheelchair also meant that Shadow Gale was the only one between the two of them who could get anything done. Just thinking about it, it seemed like a rough time. Nokko surmised that was part of the reason Pfle had gathered them all for the area unlocking quest. But Pfle's expression showed no pain or suffering, and she didn't have dirty clothes or wounds everywhere or anything else that might make her seem pitiful. It was like she was flaunting how Shadow Gale was ferrying her around as if it were just the way things should be.

If anything, the one who looked tired was the one doing the carrying. The weight of one girl was no burden to a magical heroine. But carrying her while also fighting dangerous monsters and protecting her had to be exhausting.

"Now then, it seems everyone is here," Pfle announced. All the magical girls, aside from Genopsyko Yumenoshima, were gathered at the entrance to the subterranean town. Pfle looked around, eyeing each and every one of them in turn, until finally she nodded toward Nokko. "Well then, follow me. I'll explain this area unlock quest." On Pfle's orders, Shadow Gale set off at a walk, and they all followed.

The subterranean area was basically a cave. The walls were made of hard, angular rocks. It was damp, and many places were wet from the water dripping from above. If you were careless, you might slip, so Nokko took firm steps. She could hear the sound of all their shoes tapping as they walked. With such a big crowd, the drumming was pretty loud. There was one magical girl who didn't wear any—Clantail—but her hooves were louder than footwear. What's more, compared with the wasteland, grasslands, and mountains, the path was narrow, and they couldn't walk abreast. They were forced to make their way along in single file.

From her position as second-to-last, Nokko peered up at the front. It was a continuous view of magical girls' backs. They all looked entirely defenseless. Weren't they thinking about how one of them had malicious intent and might attack them from behind? Or was that actually on their minds, and that was why they were exposing their backs—as an attempt to lure that person out?

They walked on for a while until the march stopped. Pfle called out, "Ahead is the pathway leading to the stage of the area unlock quest! An extremely dangerous enemy will be present there! Everyone, stay on guard!" She pulled a pair of glasses out of her magical phone. They were simple in design, functional-seeming, entirely without ornament, and not very magical girl–like. Without a word, Pfle put them. Sure enough, they looked terrible on her. "Now then, come follow me," she ordered, and Shadow Gale started walking. With some detailed orders ("A little more to the right—yes, right there"), Shadow Gale walked straight forward toward the wall, hit it, and then was sucked silently inside.

While all the other magical girls were voicing their surprise, Pfle popped her head out of the wall and said, "You can enter through here. It's very narrow, so take care not to bump yourself."

Clantail, second in line, cautiously touched her hand to the wall. Her fingertips, wrist, and arm passed through the wall and out of sight. The wall was fake, like an illusion or a hologram, and beyond it was a passageway. That had to mean that Pfle's glasses were an item that could see through the false barrier.

The line began to move again. Clantail entered the wall, and those after her followed. Nokko touched her hand to it as well. Without meeting any resistance, she came out to the other side.

"Wow. It only look like real rock wall," said @Meow-Meow.

Just ahead of her, Nokko nodded in response to the remark and continued on. For just an instant, her vision darkened, but when she was on the other side, she saw a passage. Unlike the cave they'd been walking through so far, this passage had the look of something artificially carved. The walls, ceiling, and floor were all parallel, and the walls met the floor and ceiling at precise and even ninety-degree angles. The walls felt smooth compared with the plain, bare rock from before. There were torches set at regular intervals along the way, and when Nokko moved her hand close to one, she felt heat. It was real fire. Magical girls didn't need illumination to see in the dark, but it still felt like something to rely on, somehow.

The hidden passage continued on from that point about five hundred steps, and then the echo of the footsteps before her changed. At Nokko's height, she couldn't see ahead, so she poked her head out to the side. The torches were positioned lower on the walls. There were stairs.

The stairs were, just like the passage, artificial. They were not at all like anything naturally occurring. They didn't go straight forward but curved very gradually to the right. To the right, more right, and yet farther right. It was a downward spiral staircase, turning clockwise.

They had to have descended two hundred steps. Taking into consideration how they'd been underground to begin with, that meant this was quite deep. Perhaps it was Nokko's imagination, but it seemed to be getting warmer, and the air was thicker and harder to breathe. At the bottom of the stairs, they arrived at a massive open space. It was even bigger than the dragon spawn locations in the subterranean area—more than two or three times greater, perhaps.

The ground was stone-paved, and the walls, unlike the passage and stairway, were bare, angular rock. The ceiling was high, easily a hundred yards up. In the center of the cavern was a raised area like a steep cliff. When Nokko saw the creature there, she gasped. Shocked noises escaped some of the other girls, and some froze in place. Their reactions were various, but they were all stunned.

"So this is the situation." Pfle turned to them and shrugged. Partially because of the glasses, she looked sillier than necessary.

Nokko took a deep breath in and out.

The raised central platform was circular, about twenty yards in diameter, and on it lay a gigantic, sleeping creature. If you were to stretch out its curled-up tail and measure its whole length, it could be fifteen yards long. Every single one of its scales was so large, shining with red, metallic luster, that Nokko could pick them all out from where they stood. Even with its mouth closed, its fangs were visible from the outside. They were so big and long—and, from what she could see, sharp. Its wings were appropriately large for its size, but there was no way such a massive body could fly in the sky. Its claws were about as long as Nokko was tall, appearing big enough to tear one to shreds in just a single swipe.

This dragon was massive. Compared with this, the creatures they'd been hunting in the subterranean area were pretenders. It was larger, but also more dragon-like. It opened its eyes wide and looked toward them. Its pupils were long, vertical, and narrow. In its gaze and bearing, Nokko could sense its hostility and lethal intent. Her legs trembled.

"You see that red line there?" Pfle pointed. When Nokko looked, she saw a red line running along maybe thirty yards from the dragon. It surrounded the creature's position at an even distance. "When you go beyond that line…"

Shadow Gale picked up a fist-sized rock from the ground at her feet and tossed it at the dragon. Instantly, the dragon opened its sizable maw, showing them its rows of exposed, carnivorous fangs. There was a red glow in the depths of its throat, and then a great fireball burst out, hitting the rock and swallowing it up as it continued to shoot toward them. Nokko jumped to the side, while some of the others threw themselves to the ground and others raised their shields. But the fireball didn't pass the red line. It just vanished in midair. Still on guard, they all breathed deep sighs. The rock hadn't been burned to ash—it was entirely gone.

"This is how it attacks," explained Pfle. "Fortunately, its attacks don't pass the red line."

Nokko wasn't the only one thinking, *So then tell us that first!* The glares needling Pfle spoke more eloquently than words.

"Take a look over there, too." Pfle pointed to the rope ladder that hung above the dragon. It went up to the ceiling, where there was a hole just barely big enough for one person to get through. "The hints we've gathered indicate that hole is the gate to the next area. And in order to get there"—Pfle's finger lowered to point to the dragon—"it seems we'll have to eliminate our dragon friend doing his best over there."

"There's no way we can beat that!" Rionetta yelled hysterically. "Did you just see that? If something like that hits us, we'll end up as black smudges! And that colossal size! Those clearly hardened scales! Punch and kick that all you like, our attacks aren't going to do a bloody thing!"

Detec Bell muttered painfully, "If Cherna were here..."

"Why talk of people who are gone?" snapped Rionetta. "Everyone here is done for."

"That's not certain at all," said Pfle. "It seems the road to completion has been prepared for us, after a fashion." Her magical phone in hand, Pfle swiped the screen. "Everyone, boot up your monster encyclopedias. This creature's data is listed there."

Opening up the monster encyclopedia, Nokko found the data there. It was called the Great Dragon, a simple name without any sort of pretension or attempt at wit. Though it was listed in the encyclopedia, most of the entry was question marks. Its methods of attack, drop items, etc., were all hidden.

"I suppose this is what they call a midgame boss," commented Pfle. "Most of its information is hidden. But some parts are displayed." The name of the monster, its spawn point, and that its element was fire—those things weren't hidden. "Its element is fire, so if we equip water charms, we'll be able to increase our damage dealt as well as reduce damage taken. Well, taking a direct hit would still mean instant death, though."

"So then what point is there to that?!" Rionetta demanded.

"*If* you take a direct hit. If you're equipped with a water charm and guarding your front with a Shield +5, you'll avoid instant death. You'll suffer some burns, but you'll survive it." Shadow Gale nodded. She must have experimented with this herself. Pfle continued. "And then there's this." She pulled a blade out of her magical phone. The small dagger seemed easy to wield, though it had a fairly low attack power. "The Dragon-Killer. It deals especially high damage to dragon-type monsters. The Item Encyclopedia explains that one strike with this weapon will kill it. We went through some trouble to acquire this, but that's irrelevant now."

Pfle then added, "Also, @Meow-Meow."

"What?"

"What exactly is the range of your talismans? If you were to attack with a building, even a dragon wouldn't go unscathed."

@Meow-Meow frowned a little. She might have been remembering crushing the samurai girl with that building. "...I just throw talisman. So I have to get really close."

"Yes, of course. Then we just have to attack from two angles. The Dragon-Killer from the right, and you from the left, @Meow-Meow. Then if either reaches the dragon, it's victory for us."

Nokko pondered Pfle's instructions. The dragon's attacks would not be fatal. They outnumbered it by a wide margin. The dragon was massive, but it seemed to lack maneuverability due to its size. If they surrounded it with a crowd, it might just work out. They had two attacks that were sure to kill it, and if either of them connected, they could win. It was dangerous, but they had to defeat this monster in order to proceed to the next area, so the players would probably choose to fight.

"Can I ask one thing?" Clantail raised her right hand. "Water charms aside, we don't have enough Shield +5 for everyone. I'm the only one in our party who has one."

"Our party doesn't have any Shield +5, either," said Lazuline. "Shields and stuff are heavy."

"We only have one Shield +5," said @Meow-Meow.

"That's fine. We have extras." Pfle raised up her own magical phone. "I won't be stingy and say I'll just lend them to you. I relinquish these free of charge."

"That's quite kind of you," said Rionetta, "but can we assume there's some condition?"

"I want the area unlock reward," said Pfle. "Specifically, I want all the candy and the real money as my own." Such an uncomplicated demand silenced them all. All sound but the dragon's nasal breathing disappeared from the great underground cavern. "You don't mind? Since Shadow Gale and I were the ones who found the way to this point."

"It's asking too much."

"The real money is a million yen, isn't it? That's quite a sum. The greedy will die first, you know."

"No matter how you look at it, taking all the bonbons is a huge rip-off."

"Maybe tone it down a little…"

Complaints leaped from each mouth, and Pfle pouted in disapproval. "The area would be unlocked. What does the reward matter?"

"If the reward doesn't matter, then you should stop tryin' to take it all for yourself! Give us the candy!" insisted Lazuline.

Rionetta added, "We don't want you getting the outrageous idea that you can put us to work without any recompense."

"You leave me no choice," Pfle said. "Fine. Then the reward for completion will be split evenly between everyone here. But if the dragon drops an item, it will be mine. Agreed?" It had to drop an item. And if there was only one, then only one of them could take it. If any among them had the right to take it, would it not be Pfle?

Everyone shot their party members meaningful glances.

"Fine."

"Under those condition."

"We'll go with that." Clantail, @Meow-Meow, and Detec Bell all agreed on behalf of their parties.

Pfle's expression of disapproval instantly vanished, and she put on a beaming smile. "Well then, let's begin the operation. Those who don't have shields, come get them. Further discussion will be needed regarding positioning. I imagine you'd all be fine with the brave magical girls in the vanguard receiving a greater portion of the reward than the rest? Also, regarding who is to hold the Dragon-Killer..." Gleefully, Pfle began giving directions.

They all moved to their positions, waiting on standby with their toes just about touching the red line. Nokko wasn't used to equipment like the shield, and it felt like an even larger burden than it actually was. But that also made it feel more reliable. When the time came, it should protect her.

Beside Nokko was the magical girl in white who was from Clantail's party...Pechka. She was trembling. Perhaps Nokko was somehow fated to end up with this girl, as she was always nearby at times like these for some reason. From what Nokko could tell, she didn't seem all that reliable.

Clantail had the Dragon-Killer in her right hand and a Shield +5 ready in her left. @Meow-Meow was straight ahead of the dragon, also with a Shield +5. The other girls were each equipped with her own Shield +5, too. Only Melville was charged with support fire using her bow and harpoons. Water charms hanging from all their necks, they encircled the dragon.

While the magical girls were getting ready, the dragon observed them with half-lidded eyes without paying much attention. It seemed bored, as if it believed that no matter how much the humans prepared, it would never lose.

Shadow Gale lowered Pfle down onto a rock and headed to her own position.

"Now then..." Pfle was right about to give the signal for the operation to begin, when—

"Huh?" Rionetta stood up. She opened her mouth, eyes turning to the entrance of the great cavern. Nokko followed her gaze. Standing there was Genopsyko Yumenoshima.

"Genopsyko!" @Meow-Meow yelled, shooting to her feet. Her expression changed from shock to joy, sparking with the elation of finally having found the person she was searching for all this time.

Her visor was up, and they had a good view of her face. She was just like she had been before—no scars like what Detec Bell's party had seen. Had she healed up already? Or had she never had anything like that to begin with?

Genopsyko was smiling, too. She spread both arms and ran over to give @Meow-Meow a big hug. Grinning as well, @Meow-Meow hugged her back, the two of them tumbling over the red line—and then the dragon spewed flame.

Before they could grasp what had just happened, the dragon spat another fireball that hit the fallen pair. Raising its head up to the ceiling, the creature's throat rumbled as it howled. The great cavern resounded.

"Never ye stop! Chaerge!" cried Melville.

With a jerk, they all moved into action.

MASTER SIDE #5

"Fal?"

No voice responded to the girl's call.

"Faaal?"

The room was dead silent. The magical phone was still off and didn't activate. The corners of the girl's mouth quirked into a little smile, one that might warrant the label "twisted." She reached out to the magical phone, stopped right before touching it, then picked up the glasses beside it and hooked them over her ears. "I'm always so busy taking them off and putting them on again! By the way, you're not gonna reply, Fal?"

In contrast with the shining monitors dotting the room, the magical phone remained silent.

"Sulking because you feel like you've betrayed your master? If that's what's bothering you, don't worry about it." The girl rolled up the sleeves of her white coat. The lab coat was two sizes too big for her, and the sleeves were rolled up three times and held with clips. "That's part of why you caught my eye. Did you know? Of all the digital fairy-type familiars, the FA series is the one with security defects. Now that they've sent out that update patch, ostensibly, there's no more defective units going around, but you haven't installed the patch yet, have you, Fal? That's why

I figured you'd betray your master, at least. Besides, you had this one predecessor—really out of this world—who wanted to see a magical-girl battle royal, no matter what it took, and tempted a master into it. Compared with that, you're a little cupcake, Fal. I took it for granted that you'd go against the will of your master and tattle on me to the Magical Kingdom. And if they were going to come try to persuade me, I figured that the one they'd send in would be you..."

The door was violently slammed open, and there stood a magical girl in white. The other girl smiled at her and, with her sleeves rolled up, beckoned her into the room. "Welcome to my world. It's good to meet you, Snow White."

Afterword

Magical girls again today, and my bowl of rice is delicious!

It's been a long time. I'm Asari Endou. This time, the story is separated into two parts. I thought that only the second part would get an afterword, but right now, I'm writing an afterword for the first part. S-mura-san, my editor, said, "I definitely never said anything like that." So maybe I dreamed it because I wanted it to be true. In S-mura-san's own words: "Just scribble off something. In the next hour."

Presently, an hour and a half has passed since I received that call.

What should I write? I love magical girls. No, maybe I shouldn't go with that. Nobody wants me to go on about *Majokko Daisakusen* bondage stuff.

Now that I think of it, once, for my elementary school graduation essay, I didn't have anything to write, so I filled up the lines with game passwords. I will endeavor to fill this with meaningful words to show that I have grown a little bit since elementary school, at least. I wasn't told not to write an afterword full of antisocial material, either, but I can exercise that much judgment on my own. Yes, I have matured!

Because I've matured, I can now pride myself on my fantastic powers of concentration. As soon as the idea of mahjong flits into my mind, I'll find myself playing it online, so I've deleted my account and password. Against my better judgment, I also end up playing free-to-play games online, so I gave my accounts to a friend. When I'm connected to the Internet, I end up wasting my time, so I pulled out my phone charger and said to my family, "Under no circumstances should you give this back to me for three days, even if I beg and cry for you to return it." Thanks to this, my phone couldn't be reached, and S-mura-san had a hard time.

As a result of all this self-control, I finished this book. I did my best.

The previous book was set in a city where the magical girls did their work—or were killed before they could do their work. But in this book, they're killing and being killed inside a game. And rather than the more straightforward killing in Volume 1, all the killing is going on covertly, in secret. "This sort of secret killing is nice, too, isn't it?" I say, complimenting my own book.

Oh, and in the second part, they'll be killing one another in even more dramatic ways. If you're thinking, "I want it to be even more over the top!" I'm sure you would do well to read part two!

Now then, let us meet again next month. I'll go take out that phone charger now.

The mystery deepens as the magical girls
lose their lives one by one in a bloody game.

What is the master's ultimate plan?

And will anyone come to save them?

Magical Girl
Raising Project
restart

AVAILABLE SPRING 2018!

Who will survive...?